R -

The Bolas

Will Chalk and his partner set out to deliver horses to a US Army post near the New Mexico border. But when they meet a fellow Texan being troubled by a ruthless land-grabber, their thoughts of returning home are put aside.

From the timberline of Condor Pass, Bruno Ogden is defiling the ranchland of Hog Flats to such an extent that grazing livestock becomes impossible. Furthermore, in nearby White Mesa, a few influential townsfolk are also involved in a dramatic scheme to drive ranchers off their land, and that includes Mollie Broad and her waterless ranch.

When unnecessary and cowardly killings take place, Will suddenly finds himself involved. With his tough old partner and a couple of loyal Bluestem workers, he attempts to turn the tables on Ogden and the spread of his Bolas company. But Will knows that mercenary gunfighters are more dangerous opponents than cowboys and hoe-men.

The Bolas

Caleb Rand

A Black Horse Western

ROBERT HALE

© Caleb Rand 2019
First published in Great Britain 2019

ISBN 978-0-7198-2941-3

The Crowood Press
The Stable Block
Crowood Lane
Ramsbury
Marlborough
Wiltshire SN8 2HR

www.bhwesterns.com

Robert Hale is an imprint
of The Crowood Press

Typeset by
Derek Doyle & Associates, Shaw Heath
Printed and bound in Great Britain by
4Bind Ltd, Stevenage, SG1 2XT

1

'There's near twenty wakin' hours in my day an' most o' them's trouble,' the proprietor of Todo Mercantile complained. He stepped around the end of the counter, lowered some fingers into the pickling jar and drew out a colourless egg. 'I don't need more,' he added, dabbing excess vinegar to the sleeve of his shirt.

The man opened his mouth and thumbed in the egg, chewed four or five times, blinked hard and swallowed. 'How'm I supposed to make business by free handin' supplies to every starve-out ranch in Hog Flats? With respect, Miss Broad, you're already in deep enough. Perhaps you should be sellin' on.'

'I'll set fire to it all before I do that,' Mollie Broad replied.

'Right now, that won't take much more'n a match,' Preston Mower commented with a smirk.

The refusal of credit came as a shock to Mollie. She stared mutely at the trader, considered a few words that might influence his sense of right and wrong, if not the reality. The man's lucrative store was piled high with hardware and consumables. Bolts of calico, hand tools, candy boxes and syrup barrels. Aromas of cheese, smoky hams and tobacco infused the pungent atmosphere.

'See sense.' Mower's lips puckered as his tongue worked at lingering fragments of dry yolk. 'Bolas will buy you out, or run you out. Ogden won't even make a tally. If I was you, I'd accept their offer an' start over.' There was no consideration, only a taunt in his voice. 'There's land near the border, an' those *señores* are practically givin' it away. Heard tell they'll even throw in a pig an' a goat to get you started.'

Mollie watched him. The man was big and out of shape, the signs crumpled across his pasty features. She knew he was eager for trouble.

'We've all had problems through this dry spell, and Bluestem's paid its way,' she said.

Mower moved over to the window and watched a small herd of horses being driven into the corrals. 'Not for a moon or two it hasn't,' he replied glibly.

Mollie chewed her top lip. The skin under her eyes was dark and her arms and hands were tacky with perspiration. She smoothed down the front of her dress, shuddered inwardly. 'I'll never sell. Not to him or anyone else,' she said.

'So, I'll give you a hundred dollars for the brand,' Mower half closed his eyes as he replied. 'I reckon it'll take more'n an overnight shower to refresh Bluestem. The weather's agin you, an' Bruno Ogden won't rest till he's driven his beef plumb into White Mesa. Hah, he wants a cattle trail an' a turnpike . . . even a goddamn railroad, an' he wants *you* out o' the way, lady.'

'I know. But I've got the advantage of being here already.' Mollie's voice carried a slight tremor, but also a touch of anger.

The mercantile door pinged its bell on opening. A man stood in the doorway, framed against the light. 'Which one of you's Preston Mower?' he asked, smiling at Mollie. 'We've brought in some horses.'

'Yeah, I saw,' Mower answered and turned back to Mollie. 'Look, Ogden's organizing a trail herd. He's mad as a peeled rattler . . . ready to fight anyone who tries to stop him from makin' it to the shippin' pens.'

'Your pens, Mr Mower.' Mollie gritted her teeth. She felt a sudden chill in the room, and knew the man behind her must be curious at the exchange.

Mower spread his hands and shrugged. 'I'm just warnin' you.'

'I'm a Texican. And that usually means taking threats badly.' Mollie raised her chin, fixed her gaze on the trader. 'If your friend Ogden has a notion to make a fight of it, he'd best look for some other business to get into.'

'Smart words don't butter no corn,' Mower answered back as Mollie walked from the store. 'Take my word for it, he'll make things so tough for you an' your Bluestem, you'll settle for ten cents on the dollar.'

As Mollie walked from the store the stranger held a folded docket out to Mower. 'Some are mine . . . the horses,' he said. 'I was told you'd pay me separate.'

Mower read quickly. 'An' you'll be William Chalk?' he enquired, eyeing the gunbelt and walnut grip of a .44 Navy Colt.

'Yeah, I'm him,' the man replied, turning to watch the street. He saw Mollie snatch off her bonnet, settle onto the narrow seat of an elderly pie buggy.

Mower screwed up his eyes again. 'Can you drive a dozen head on to Condor Pass? Ogden's waitin' on 'em.'

Chalk shook his head. 'No. I don't rightly know where that is, but it ain't where we're going.'

'We?'

'My partner. He's at the pens.'

Mower silently considered a moment. 'Well, how about signin' up with Ogden?' he asked. 'It'll be fightin' wages.

There's a land fight in the offin' an' he could use a few more guns.'

'Against who?'

'Bluestem.'

'The woman who just left?' Chalk raised a near incredulous smile. 'I'm from Littlefield, mister, so that makes me a beef head too. We don't make our way in the world by fighting each other.'

'I should've tagged you for a gunhawk the moment you stepped in here.' Suddenly there was a shade of mean approval in Mower's eyes. 'You a mite proddy about somethin'?'

'No, not yet. And I'm not a paid gun.' Chalk glanced at the egg jar, thought better of it, and stepped towards the biscuit barrel. He dipped his hand, ignored the look from Mower. 'Just pay me for the stock and I can ride on.'

'Sure. Whatever you want.' Mower turned on his heel, went into the office at the rear of the store. He returned a minute later with a slim wad of banknotes. 'Four hundred an' fifty dollars,' he stated curtly. 'If you'll just sign the bill o' sale.'

'It's five hundred.' Chalk made no attempt to take the money. 'That's what's on the invoice.'

With his eyes now glinting with irritation, Mower glared at Chalk. He waved the notes. 'Four fifty,' he repeated.

'If reading's not your problem, what is it mister? I said where I was from, and that don't make me an Okie halfbake. If you're balky about the cost, I'll just take them somewhere else.'

In a moment or two of silence the two men glared at each another. 'There ain't anywhere else,' Mower started. 'Ogden buys from me . . . for Bolas. Other outfits are too broke to purchase stock they can't even water.'

'But you can.' Distaste was now edging into Chalk's

8

voice. 'That paper says five hundred dollars, an' that's what I want . . . not a red cent less.'

Mower was a harsh, unprincipled trader, but he had a wry appreciation of Chalk's hold-out. He knew Bruno Ogden needed the horses, was reliant on them. 'The full five then. Hell, there's already too many chiselers round here,' he grudgingly conceded. 'In case you hadn't already noticed, Hog Flats is hard land to dig over. Not much in the way o' horseback work either. Bolas is big enough to carry the trouble, though.'

'What is this Bolas?' Chalk asked.

'Bruno Ogden's Land an' Stock Company. Like I said, he'll be payin' top rates.'

'Yeah, for guns,' Chalk reminded Mower. 'Right now I'm a dollar-a-day man. Be a chill in Hades afore I'm advised by a horse thief.'

Mower forced out a thin smile. 'So try Bluestem. They're goin' to need all the help they can get, but they'll probably find your rate a bit sharp. Head west when you leave town. You won't miss 'em.'

Chalk looked uncomprehendingly at the trader, dropped a hard doughboy into a shirt pocket, then stepped outside. He looked out at the road in the direction Mollie Broad had driven, then he walked to the corrals.

Latchford Loke was shoving his way through the snorty throng of horses, cuffing their noses as they tried to bite him. He was older than Chalk, and carried the colour and wiriness of a seafaring man.

'We've got work,' Chalk said, shading his eyes against the sun as it breached the distant San Andreas Mountains.

'Did you get the dollars?' Loke climbed through the pole bars of the corral, stumbled to the ground and cursed as a fleabit grey snatched at his leg. 'Son-of-a-bitch. If I'd

9

got some cutters I'd yank them goddamn teeth from its thick head, so help me.'

'I know you would, Latch,' Chalk replied none too sincerely. 'But let's go eat. Then we can push on before dark.'

'Push on?' Latch exclaimed. 'Where to? Hell, Will, we're always in a goddamn hurry. I reckoned on stayin' the night, an' there's the Bello Hotel across the street. I'm gettin' so dry I'll soon be spittin' cotton.'

'From what I've just heard, there's going to be trouble hereabouts, Latch.' Chalk briefly told of Preston Mower's idea of a job offer and Latch bristled with offence.

'Sounds more like a cat fight than a range war, but still somethin' to stay away from, if you ask me.' Latch bent his head enquiringly, met the shadowed eyes of his partner. 'I reckon it's 'cause o' the girl. We get ourselves into a nice trade an' you want to blow it wide open,' the man voiced his indignation. 'Why the hell can't we stick to broncs . . . cattle even? They're not half so much trouble.'

'It's called Bluestem.' Will recalled the name which had been burnt into a side panel of Mollie Broad's old wagon. 'And the lady's from Texas,' he added a tad weaker.

'Hah, should o' known.' Latch slapped dust from the front of his clothes. 'But I'm not fightin' for more than I have to, or gettin' paid for.' He spat dryly, cursed again and muttered. 'Just one settler for Chris'sakes. I ain't ever been anywhere called Bello.'

'You have, Latch. But probably never knew it.' Will grinned. 'Just one, then.'

From the window of his mercantile, Preston Mower watched the two men. William Chalk's confident determination still annoyed him. *If he goes up against Ogden, he'll get his edge dulled* he thought, and turned away.

10

2

From the porch of her ranch house, Mollie Broad first saw the grullo mare and its slumped rider walking from the wash. Knowing it was Lewis Redbone returning from his exploring of Cholla Creek, she rushed down the veranda steps.

Henri, the French-Cree metis, was already halfway across the home yard. He was shouting, stretching his arms as if to catch Redbone if he fell from the saddle.

With clenched fists, Ben Shoeville was cursing as he ran past Mollie. 'Get him into the house,' he barked as the figure wilted, and rolled silently towards the hard-packed dirt. Mollie saw the bloodied shoulder, the dark stain that filled the front of Redbone's shirt. 'Get him to my room, Henri,' she instructed anxiously.

'Don't bother.' Redbone opened his eyes, and with a thick tongue attempted to lick his lips. His face was grey and furrowed with pain, and a bubble of blood appeared from the corner of his mouth.

Shoeville dropped to his knees, eased the sodden shirt material from Redbone's belt. He stared grimly at the bullet wound and mumbled more curses. Then he looked up at Henri and shook his head.

Redbone's legs drew in slightly and his chest gave a

11

shallow heave. His eyes searched out Mollie who, unable to figure more useful words, was just staring at him.

'Who was it, Lew? Who shot you?' Shoeville asked.

Redbone turned his face towards the ranch house, then north and south across the sun-baked land.

Shoeville took a water bottle from Henri and poured a trickle onto Redbone's lips. 'Tell us who it was, Lew. Just give us a name,' he said. 'We'll take care of it for you.'

Redbone blinked long and hard. 'Didn't see 'em. But they're wirin' the valley,' he rasped, and closed his eyes for the last time.

Mollie moved a step back, looked reluctantly at Henri and Shoeville. 'No more,' she started, bitter and quiet. 'Take your pick of the horses and pull out before Bolas rides in. Unless you both want to end up facing dirt, it's the best . . . all I can offer you.'

'Like hell.' Shoeville was influenced by the time Broad was a big name, a power in Hog Flats. 'This neck o' the woods ain't up for sale yet, ma'am. We got to chug through it. You, me an' Henri. If we all stick it out, who knows?'

'I know that very soon you'll both come back roped to your saddles like my pa.' Mollie lifted a hand towards the dark pine spires of Condor Pass, the snow-capped peaks beyond. 'Sure, we're not for sale. But why? For what? Bluestem's becoming one hell-of-a-size graveyard.'

'Well, your pa would be climbing out of it, if he could hear that kind of surrender talk.' Wanting to arouse the fighting spirit of the Broads, the man's words were intentionally harsh. Shoeville watched Mollie, saw a likeness of Elmer Broad in the set of her jaw line, her small hands tough from the drag of hogging ropes.

'Surrender?' Mollie repeated scathingly. 'In less than a year, Bluestem's been stripped to the bone. Surrender's got nothing to do with it. There's nothing left, for God's sake.'

'Then it'll take the three of us to fight . . . to bring it back.' Shoeville got to his feet. He stood straight, drew his shoulders back. Twenty-five years ago Elmer Broad had brought him to Bluestem after rescuing him from the grip of border cow thieves. To Ben Shoeville's way of thinking, there was still a debt needed repaying. He snorted right-eous anger, staring off towards Condor Pass. It was where Bruno Ogden's Land and Stock Company had its holdings, and the thought pounded him like a steam hammer.

As for the ranch, Mollie Broad had fought a losing battle against nature, its overwhelming forces. Bluestem was now part of a barren wasteland. Along the creeks, juniper and willow were beginning to droop their branches above rock and dry gravel. For a long year, dry winds from the north had ripped at the planks of the barn, warping wagon wheels, driving powdered dirt through cracks, deep into axle bearings. The last vestiges of anything green and succulent had been stripped from the land. Beyond all this, the shimmering sun-baked crags of Condor Pass rose up against a blue sky, a barrier to water and grass.

Mollie returned Shoeville's stark look, smiled tiredly at Henri and shrugged. 'You know I've no need for you or Henri any more, Ben. I've no money to pay either of you . . . even back wages. Take the shave-tails and ride east . . . north to Santa Fe, maybe.'

Shoeville dismissed the suggestion with a wave of his hand. 'With respect Miss Mollie, I'll leave when I'm good an' ready. An' that ain't just yet,' he retorted. 'That proba-bly goes for Henri, too.'

'You did Pa's bidding, you can do mine,' Mollie snapped back. She understood the significance and purpose of what Shoeville was saying, but was too crushed to accept readily. 'I asked Preston Mower to help us through the summer,' she said, endorsing her memory of events. 'I told him the creeks would fill when the rains came, but he turned me down. It made no difference that I didn't already owe him. Then he practically ran me from the store.'

'Goddamn jumped-up peddler,' Shoeville said angrily, turning away as he heard the sound of approaching riders. A moment later he threw a warning glance at Mollie and Henri when someone called out his name.

He recognized two of the riders as Far Creek waddies, but the other three were Bolas. They were the hired guns of Bruno Ogden, wanting to look disruptive and dangerous.

'What are you wantin', Deavis?' Shoeville called back. 'Ridin' in here mob-handed?'

'You should keep this side o' the Far Creek markers,' Mal Deavis replied, his lips stretching across darkly stained teeth. 'Then maybe you've been told already,' he added, his eyes halting momentarily on the body of Redbone.

'Careful you don't make another mistake.' Shoeville ignored Mollie, looked hard at the other two Bolas men. They were dressed commanchero, most likely renegade traders from the Llano with prices on their heads. 'Next time we won't be meetin' you empty handed. Now *you've* been told.'

One of the Far Creek cowhands heeled his horse forward. He nodded at Mollie, his face strained with unease. 'Far Creek's sold out to Bolas,' he said. 'We meant to come here alone. There's still some silver in the Casa Grande . . . thought we'd give it a try.'

'Oh no! You can't.' Mollie groaned aloud, held out her hand imploringly. She knew that if Far Creek was appropriated by Bolas, all movement south and east would be controlled by Ogden.

'Well, they have.' Deavis dribbled a thin stream of tobacco juice, raised his eyes to Mollie. 'We tried to tell your man, but he wanted to make a fight of it.' He grinned meanly. 'You need more'n trail hands to hold down this land, lady.'

'Lew Redbone never made a fight of it,' Shoeville fumed. 'He was shot twice with a rifle.' Age had tempered Ben Shoeville, but anger now hardened his features. 'The murderous scum who pulled the trigger didn't even have to get close,' he challenged bitterly.

Henri turned his back contemptuously to the gunmen, walked over towards Mollie. 'Best if you go back to the house, Miss Mollie. There's little you can do here,' he said.

'An' pack your traps,' Deavis snorted. 'But leave your tally sheets . . . you won't have need.'

'You've one minute to get off this land, mister.' Shoeville's voice was now steely, uncompromising. 'Ride in here again, an' I'll blow you from the saddle.'

One of the commancheros held up his hand, looked at Deavis and shook his head menacingly. 'We were told to make no trouble,' he said.

'You've not said what you *did* come here to make,' Shoeville returned.

'An offer. Hands are needed at Far Creek. Mr Ogden said you would be the best available man.'

'Yeah? Well I'm already that here.'

The commanchero shrugged. 'If you say so,' he said, and gathered in his reins. As the man and his cohorts prepared to move away, Shoeville took a step towards them.

'There's probably Bluestem beef that's strayed on to Far Creek,' he said.

'You been told to stay away from there.' Deavis hauled his horse around, his gun hand nearest Shoeville.

Disregarding the Bolas man, Shoeville continued. 'The brush must be full o' Bluestem stuff. I'm bringin' it all back home.'

15

'How?' Deavis once more bared his dirty teeth.

'They're our mavericks an' I've a right. I'll use a gun against anyone who tries to stop me.'

Deavis jerked his head towards the body of Redbone. 'Then you'll likely get what *he* got.' He looked beyond the Bluestem ranch house towards the White Mesa road. 'Right now this looks a real popular place, an' a crowd ain't company,' he said, indicating that the Bolas commancheros follow him.

Without further words, the two men from the Far Creek ranch also walked their horses in the direction of the town road. But they headed west, not east. Shoeville watched them for a few moments, wondered what would have happened if he'd goaded the Bolas riders into more than threats.

When two new riders swung off the town trail and cantered towards them, Shoeville turned and signalled to Henri. He eyed the dusty figures, tried to place them, give them a brand.

'Name yourself,' he challenged, stepping between them and Mollie.

'William Chalk.' A four days' growth of beard shrouded Will's face. He glanced quickly at Redbone's body, then out at the three men who were riding on to the dry wash. His eyes read tiredness and his shoulders slackened as he drew rein.

'Latchford Loke. How'd you do,' Latch said, lifting his hat towards Mollie.

'Got yourselves lost?' Mollie walked up to them 'Missed the big trail road I expect. Still,' she continued nervously, 'You're more than welcome to share what we haven't got.'

Will frowned, looked at the ranch house. He noted the wind-scoured barns and empty corrals, what appeared to be a starved-out business.

16

'Is this Bluestem?' he asked quietly.

'Used to be. What's it to you?'

'Feller back in town said you needed hands . . . helping hands.' Will dragged the sleeve of his lower arm across his face.

'You've already had yourself a good look.' Again, Shoeville was chewing for a fight. 'Do we look like we need a helpin' hand?'

'In a manner of speaking,' Will replied, close to a grin.

'Who told you we needed help?' Mollie's cool glance stopped Shoeville saying any more.

'The mercantile man. Him you were having unaccommodating words with. You obviously don't remember me being there.'

'I do, sort of. I was mainly seeing red at the time.'

'Yes, ma'am.' Will fixed Shoeville in his stare. 'We brought in a short herd for the cavalry at Tyler's Post. Got paid off three days ago.'

'So you're hired. Henri, fix them up in the bunkhouse,' Mollie directed.

Shoeville said nothing as Mollie brushed past him and walked to the house. He waited, spoke up when the door had shut. 'I reckon you'd best ride on. Head for Condor Pass. Bruno Ogden will fix you up.'

Will climbed slowly from the saddle of his buckskin mare. He looked at the body of Redbone, stared soberly at the wound. 'With respect feller, *you* don't know what's best for me.'

Shoeville struggled to keep his anger in check. 'There's not enough for us. Even the vermin's leavin' for Chris'sakes. No water, no grub. Nothin'.'

Will looked at Henri. 'Lady said for you to make some space for us. But if you've got another shovel, I'll help you dig a hole. This heat won't improve him.'

'I'm tellin' you, there's nothing to be made here,' Shoeville persisted. 'We ain't even got stock currency.' He indicated Redbone with a jerk of the head. 'That's about what you'll earn by stayin'.'

Latch dismounted, exchanged reins for Henri's shovel. Then he cursed and spat. Flies had come from nowhere, hummed close to the body, the dark-stained dirt.

3

'Whatever god or goblin you believe in, they'd never have meant the end to be like this.' Henri's face was impassive, but deep hurt raged within him. He lifted his gaze from the body at his feet and stared at Will. 'You're not from these parts, are you?' he said.

Will shook his head. 'Shows, does it?'

'So it was White Mesa's good merchant Mower who sent you out here lookin' for work?' Shoeville said with continued disapproval.

'He mentioned it . . . certainly didn't *send* us out here. That was *our* decision.' Will looked beyond Shoeville, thinking that Bluestem and its land was as bleak and barren as the alkali salt pans that surrounded Tyler's Post.

'Are you stayin' or goin'?' Shoeville asked.

'We'll get off your range, if you want us to,' Will offered.

Shoeville's eyes appeared to be shut, but he was thinking, watching the nuances of Will. 'Still lookin' for work?' he asked.

Will and Latch exchanged glances. 'I guess we are,' Latch said cautiously.

'Besides, right now, no food or water and little prospect sounds plenty,' Will added.

Shoeville gave a thin smile. 'You left out hunkerin' down

19

with us.'

'How many's *us*?'

'I'm Ben Shoeville, an' this is Henri. Lew Redbone don't count any more. You understand the trouble we're in?'

'Yeah,' Will said immediately. He thought of Preston Mower, the man who had sought to separate him and Latch from fifty dollars, attempting to get them to ride up to Condor Pass, the nonsense concerning gun work in the employ of someplace called Bolas. 'Is Mower mixed up in this fight?' he asked.

'Ogden. It's just Ogden and his goddamn Bolas company.' Shoeville turned and looked towards Condor Pass, through the shimmering haze of alkali that rose from the bottom lands. 'Mower's the tempting spider. But I'm playin' a long game . . . waitin' for the moment to mash him underfoot.'

Will held out his hand. 'Suits us. Meantime, we'll help you with your planting.'

'Thanks. We'll take a backtrail tomorrow . . . find out where it happened.'

Shoeville's jaw clenched as he looked up from Redbone's body.

'But it won't be including you,' Will took off his gun belt, hung it around the saddle-horn. 'That's for Latch and me. They don't know us.'

Shoeville thought for a moment before responding, then, having considered the futility, he let out his breath and walked to the bunkhouse. Mollie was standing at the corner of the ranch-house veranda, and he stopped, tried to establish her mood before either of them spoke.

'We shouldn't have taken them on,' she said. 'Please ask them to leave in the morning.'

'They've work to do. Scoutin' along the Cholla . . . takin' a closer look at the pass.'

'You know I can't afford to take on riders,' Mollie protested. 'How are we supposed to feed them?'

'If we're to chin Bolas, there is a way.'

Mollie shot her top hand a piercing stare. 'I hope you don't mean what I think you mean, Ben.'

'Gettin' involved was their idea, Miss Mollie. It's up to them. They look old an' ugly enough to make their own decisions. But I also happen to think they're good men. Good enough, anyways.' Shoeville once more looked to the east, his mien settling firm and tough. 'I can promise you one thing,' he added determinedly. 'I'll not rest until you an' Bluestem are safe . . . up an' runnin' again.'

It was full dark when, having passed the guards at the mouth of the pass, Preston Mower rode into Bolas. The bunkhouse was in darkness, but there was low lamplight from a room in the main building. Bruno Ogden came to the main door, and called out as Mower rode up to the tie rail.

'Is that you, Deavis?'

'No. It's me. Mower.'

Ogden grunted and led the way into the house, turned up the lamplight in his richly furnished den.

'The girl came in today,' Mower said. 'Yeah, she had a list of wants, extended credit bein' one of 'em. Shame.' He produced two cigars from a top pocket. 'Courtesy of Havana an' Todo Mercantile.' He handed one to Ogden, raised the lamp globe to light the other one for himself.

Ogden placed his elbows on his desk and regarded the store keeper. 'And Far Creek came through,' he replied.

'I heard.' Mower slumped into a wing chair, was thoughtful for a moment. He contemplated the glowing tip of his cigar, then grinned. 'So what's next? Where we goin'?'

Ogden smiled coldly. 'I'm trading Bluestem for three men. Shoeville, Redbone and their Frenchman. That done, I'll run Hog Flats – the water, the beef, the graze. If any settlers want to buy in, they can farm from the bottoms. We can build a road, you can open another store.'

Mower nodded. 'Well, Bolas are sure on the up,' he commented. 'Turner Foote will be glad to hear it. Him an' Marge.'

'Huh, like a runt don't know it's a runt until there's no teat left,' Ogden offered. He leaned forward, the lamp highlighting his pale grey eyes. 'When Bluestem's gathered, I'll have just about everything that's worth having.'

The Todo Mercantile owner stared at his companion, shuddered at what sounded like the sudden onset of trouble. 'A *quarter* of everything, Bruno,' he said. 'You ain't the augur of all you survey, just yet.'

Ogden's lip curled into a chilling smile as he opened a desk drawer. Without taking his eyes off Mower, he drew out a few sheets of paper and handed them across the desk. 'A *fourth* of Bolas,' he murmured. 'The agreement says nothing about the others. Read it. I bought Far Creek with *my* money. Bluestem's going to need *my* guns.'

'Ben Shoeville won't roll over,' Mower said thickly.

Ogden laughed. 'Hah, what's it to you, Mower? Hell, you only took down Elmer Broad from lying in wait. You're expert at paying for something you wouldn't do yourself.'

Mower straightened up. 'The Bluestem crew isn't the patsy you seem to think it is. They'll fight. Besides, they've two more riders. That's two more guns.'

Ogden said nothing. He listened and the tight grin remained.

'You'll have to lodge rights of possession in Silver City,' Mower went on. 'How are you going to explain where the money came from? Are you going to tell 'em it's all from rustled Bluestem an' Far Creek stock? When Foote hears about it, he'll forget the niceties of any law. He'll say you bought out Far Creek with cash you got from the border bank heist.'

Ogden created a pretend yawn. 'What did you come here for, Mower? Is that it . . . all you've got?'

Mower bristled with annoyance. 'You're not gettin' away with this. When someone tries to rob me, you think I won't fight?' Mower threatened.

'You couldn't fight your way from a rotten flour sack, Mower.' Ogden came to his feet and shook his head. 'You started this, not me. It was *you* who brought me, then my crew into it. So go see Foote. He'll have to know sometime. But when he's in Silver City tell him to remember these.' With that, Ogden snatched the deeds from the desk and waved them at the trader. 'Tell him to remember the partnership. That's him, you and me and a spurned woman who'll eat your heart out.'

Mower closed his eyes for a moment. A rage was close to the surface, but he held his tongue. He turned his head and listened. 'Someone's just rode in,' he said.

Both men were watching the door when it opened and Deavis walked in.

'Hi, Mower,' the man said. 'You're a ways off your patch.'

Ogden sat down again, pulled out another drawer of his desk, and set out three glasses and a bottle of labelled whiskey.

Deavis took off his hat and bandanna and wiped his face. 'Redbone went ridin' today,' he announced baldly.

Ogden put the cigar in his mouth, and eyed his man. He knew Deavis liked to perform little dramas, a sort of justification for payment.

'He won't be doin' that again.' Deavis filled his glass and

23

swallowed the liquor. He rolled the glass between his fingers, looked at Mower with sneering familiarity. 'How long you been makin' night deliveries?'

'When are you talking about?' Ogden asked.

Deavis refilled his glass, took a slow turn around the room and paused behind Mower's chair. 'I just said. He came ridin' up the Cholla snoopin' an' sniffin' like a goddamn bush dog. I dropped him easy enough.'

'Him and his horse, I trust.' Ogden suggested.

Deavis hesitated: 'Was I supposed to? Shootin' broncs ain't natural,' he replied warily.

'So it ran back to Bluestem with an empty saddle. Hoofprints from the creek right to their goddamn hitch-rail.' Ogden's eyes flashed angrily. 'Like sending them a guide.'

'Well, that ain't quite what happened,' Deavis responded even more diffidently. 'I'm thinkin' he died in the saddle.'

'After he likely caught sight of the barrier work. Hell, Deavis, you've got one big horse turd for a brain. You let him see the barrier then go home to talk about it. Why didn't you tuck a little map in his pocket for good measure?'

The hired gunhand felt the sweat gathering between his shoulder blades, pulled back into the shadows of the room. 'He's dead. I watched 'em bury him.'

Hardiness drained from Preston Mower as alarm grew. He moved uneasily towards the door. 'Our agreement only covers Bolas,' he said. 'If Redbone lived long enough to talk, there's already worms in the fishpond.' He indicated the figure of Deavis in the near darkness. 'You let that loco gunman go blunderin' around your beaver works. Goddamnit, if Redbone caught sight, the Broad girl will go straight to the Land Offices. She'll have no trouble gettin' an injunction against you an' your Bolas company. Looks to me, mister, like someone's started to piss in the wind.'

'Just get out, Mower.' Ogden was seething. 'Get back to your ribbons and candy. I'll take some men on to Bluestem tomorrow . . . burn 'em out if I have to.'

Hardly taking his eyes from the two men, Mower scuttled out to his horse. He saddled anxiously and knee'd it away from the rail. He would have to inform Turner Foote and Marge Highgate about Ogden's intent, but couldn't think of a resourceful, safe way of doing it.

4

At first light, when the qualities of the ground were recognizable, Will Chalk and Latchford Loke picked up the trail of Redbone's horse. By the time early sunbeams touched the peaks of Condor Pass they were high above Bluestem. The trail headed east, away from the creek towards the cleft in the peaks.

'You realize if that's where Redbone ran into a hideaway gun, it's where *we* will?' Latch said.

'Not if we can't be seen. We'll wait until the sun moves on.' Will slowly moved his mare away from the skyline, listened intently to the sounds of silence. He was already hot and dry, and had an impulsive notion to drench himself in fresh creek water. He peered into the broken country, made out the rutted wagon road that ribboned up into the pass.

'What's that white stuff up on the peaks?' Latch asked as he rode alongside his partner.

'Snow.'

'So how come the creek's dry?'

Will looked east again at Condor Pass. The tall pikes were now bathed in a pinky golden glow, tangles of scrub pine blanketing the slopes below the snowline. He started to curse softly, his heart starting to thump at the gist of

Latch's remark, at what he'd just started to consider himself. 'Must have taken another route ... gone somewhere else,' he answered distractedly. 'We don't have to cross over. Let's head up there from this side.'

They put their horses along the foothills heading north, then turned about, swung south to the east side of the pass. An hour later they saw the grassland and the boundary marker.

At the weather-scarred board, Latch leaned sideways from his saddle. 'Far Creek,' he read aloud.

Deep among the snarls of jack pine and scrub oak, Will grunted a thoughtful response. He tried to remember every detail of the trail. Ben Shoeville had told of Far Creek selling out to Bolas. That meant they were now a long ways into rival land.

At the head of the graze lay a deserted line shack. Its planked door hung half open off strap hinges, the rear wall buckling where the wind caught at the sod roof. A mile beyond lay the end of the blind canyon, enfolding walls too steep and perilous to be scaled by man or beast. Will knew it was unwise to go any further, but he had to find out what it was that Redbone had seen, that had got him killed by a Bolas gunman.

'We'll ride for the rim,' Will said at last, mindful of the timber that screened them. They held in to cover for an hour, then dropped downslope, cutting west across Condor Pass to tawny grassland. It was here they saw their first cattle, a short mix of Far Creek and Bolas steers.

Latch cast a glance over the livestock. 'That's one way to put together a herd,' he observed. 'Dogies split from their mamas at calfin' time, an' the Bolas tally goes up.'

'And not one Bluestem maverick.' Will looked back over the trail, at the distant snowline. 'I don't understand,' he said. 'Do you suppose they've drifted up there?'

Latch had another stirring of uncertainty. 'Maybe,' he replied. 'Maybe they went lookin' for the goddamn creek-water. I think we could be steppin' into a big, flat loop.'

'So we'll pick up the headwaters of the Cholla,' Will decided. 'Bolas doesn't own the sierras.'

They spent fifteen minutes looking for signs before finding the tracks they wanted. A man had been on stake-out at the end of a rising line of rock chimneys. They saw the ashes of the fire, marks where horses had been on short picket. The trail turned south and they followed at a faster pace.

By late afternoon, the sentinel rock towers of Condor Pass loomed before them. Will took point and they dropped down into the canyon, a steep-sided valley almost a quarter mile wide. There was grama and buffalo grass, cottonwoods and willow, which circled waterholes. It was a place the drought hadn't touched, a rincon concealed and sheltered by towering peaks.

Four loose horses were grazing, but Will saw no sign of man until he came to a point where he could better look down on the camp. A man was lying on his back, an arm crooked around a Winchester rifle. His head was propped on a mossy boulder, his hat pulled down to cover his face. *Just as well . . . he'd be looking me straight in the eye, otherwise*, Will thought wryly. He held up his hand to indicate quiet, signed for Latch to remain while he went on down to talk.

Will made no secret of his arrival, let his horse clip its hoofs on their approach. Eventually the guard heard him and scrabbled to his feet, the barrel of his Winchester raised as Will picked his way across the canyon floor.

'How'do there,' the man said, a degree of uncertainty blighting his peace.

'How'do, to you,' Will replied. He edged his mare over to the pool, dismounted and knelt down to drink.

'What you doin' *here*?' the man continued.

'Taking advantage of your hospitality, first. Looking for the boys, second.' Will attempted to sound natural.

'They've gone on to the boom . . . left here some hours ago.' The guard lowered his rifle, rested the barrel against his leg. 'Don't recall seein' you around here. You new?'

'Hah, I been called a few things in my time, but bein' *new*'s not one of 'em!' Will smiled, creating an agreeable look for the man. He looked thoughtfully at the coffee pot, the greasy skillet. 'You got anything that fits this? Hell, I could eat a rolled poncho.'

'Or a fat Bluestem cow, eh?'

'Yeah. However they fall.' Will eyed the guard less openly, saw the gleam of amusement in the man's eyes.

'There's a few hundred head up there. Go help yourself,' the man said, waving a hand towards the upper canyon.

'They're all Bluestem, are they?'

'How long have you been with us?' the man questioned by way of an answer, a shadow of indecision now clouding his face. 'I don't rightly recollect seein' you around.'

Will forced himself to keep calm. He took a half-eaten corn dodger from his traps and dipped it in the old skillet grease. He took a reluctant bite, cursed inwardly when he heard the sound of Latchford Loke's horse.

He spat, raised his head as the guard swung around with his rifle. 'Hey,' he cautioned, 'we got another new hand. He's been covering my back.'

'You didn't say you'd brought someone with you,' the guard said, getting ever more wary.

'There's a lot of things I haven't said yet, mister. Should I have told you?' Will responded quickly.

The guard shrugged his shoulders. 'It could stop him from gettin' his head filled with rifle bullets.'

'The only hostile's we're likely to run into up here's black bear.' Will looked up as Latch came into view. 'Let's eat some of your chow,' he suggested. 'I'll have to catch up with the others before they get to the dam. Mr Ogden wants it done quick,' he chanced.

They ate in near silence, the guard sorting them out with slices of fried salt pork and hot coffee.

Twenty minutes later, Will hauled himself to his feet. 'What's the quickest route to this goddamn barrier?' he asked. 'I know it's our fault we've lost time, but I don't want to have to pay for it.'

'Yeah. It's just some things're more important than others.' The man stood up, pointed to a discernible trail through thickets of jack pine and scrub oak. 'Once across all that, you'll find a dry wash. Just follow it south,' he added, slowly, as though sensing there was something wrong.

Calmly, Will and Latch caught their horses and rode off slowly through the brakes. All the grazeland was now a holding of the Bolas company, and they were more alert and careful. After filling their water bottles they worked their way back down to the dry wash, rode the shaded side until they heard the roil of a cataract. Will reined in, listening, trying to visualize what lay ahead.

Latch smiled, was making the Indian sign for having sniffed fire-smoke on the wind. Then they picked up the foreground sound of approaching horses along the wash. The pair swung into the tangled willow, and watched silently as three horsemen rode by, back in the direction of the guard camp.

'Hell, we could be runnin' into more'n we came from,' Latch said, bumping his mare close alongside Will. 'You reckon this might be a time for help?'

'When we find out what they've done to the water. I

want to see for myself.'

'Personally I ain't too bothered,' Latch responded sullenly.

Without bothering to reply, Will headed his horse on along the wash towards the sound of cascading water. Less than a mile up creek they rode into the camp site. A picket line was still strung between two trees, a stretched canvas sheet between two more, but men and horses were gone. Will edged his way unhurriedly towards the column of white water, the shining halos of spray. He cursed expressively when he saw the giant cluster of branches and logs, the buttress of earth which formed the structure of the dam beneath it.

'Does that answer your question about what happened to the water?' Will looked up at Latch and shook his head. 'This is the Cholla. The beginning and the end of it.'

Latch stood in his stirrups to get a better look. 'Wouldn't have taken 'em long,' he said. 'It's annihilation for Bluestem ... those who ain't bottom o' the south slopes. It's a murderous an' cruel intent for them who's that way inclined.'

'They are,' Will breathed, letting the consequences sink in. In a swift wind-back he could see what had happened. With the flow of the Cholla feeding Bluestem's home creek, most country beyond the pass was now reverting to a barren, hostile wasteland.

Will turned away quickly when two riders emerged from the creekside willow. It was too late for him and Latch to find cover and there was no way back. Besides, the lower camp guard would have passed on the news that two strangers were at the dam.

'Sit easy,' Will said under his breath. With a hand raised in greeting he knee'd his horse towards the two men. 'That's some tired old sentry work,' he called out. 'We could've been anyone.'

The two men were those of commanchero appearance who had ridden on to Bluestem property to warn off Mollie Broad and Ben Shoeville. Pito screwed his face into a frown as he tried to place Will and Latch. 'We can still shoot you,' he returned. 'Boss said nothin' about any new men, did he. . . ?'

The second man, who was named Copper John, grunted, dropped his hand to his belted pistol. 'No. I'd have remembered. Who the hell are you gringos?'

Nobody moved, and before anyone spoke further, an agitated clamour of voices rose from the wash. Two more guards appeared and Will realized they were trapped.

'They're Bluestem. Rope 'em in,' one of the men shouted.

'Hey Latch, you remember that jump? Pickett's charge!' Will asked.

'Sure do, cap'n!' Latch answered immediately. 'Right now's as good a time as any to try again.'

Together the pair yelled, drew their Colts, jabbed with their spurs and drove their horses forward. They crashed in and out of the wash, through the startled Bolas men.

The two commancheros fought their startled mounts, swung them around, but by the time they were under control Will and Latch were into the trees.

Copper John drew his carbine, slammed the short barrel into the guard's shoulders as he rode by. 'Get to Ogden. Tell him riders have been up here,' he rasped.

A rifle bullet tore between trees, spitting bark shards as Will lay flat along his horse's neck. 'Latch,' he shouted, 'if we get separated, give Bluestem a good look before you go riding in.'

Soon they were away from the timber brakes, but bullets still buzzed the air around them. They rode for the rising ground and for an instant were more exposed to fire. Then the creek was below them and they charged on, kicked and heeled their mounts into the drop, the stretch of ice-cold water.

They were scrambling for cover on the other side when they heard Copper John calling out.

'Ride,' the Bolas commanchero yelled. 'You'll be dead meat if you don't get 'em!'

'You heard him, Latch,' Will retaliated. 'Drive to your knees if you have to. Just get away.' He cursed, and halted for a moment to lean down and drag on his cinch. He was wet, and his boots were filled with water. He knew he'd raise a blister or two before they made the comparative security of Hog Flats.

They were three miles across the slopes of Condor Pass when they saw the horsemen emerge from the timber. There were six of them now in pursuit, and Will and Latch settled down to a steady gallop across open country. They swung north, then west, staying carefully to their advantage. The horses had been revived by the fresh water and with reasonable luck Will knew they should be at least one mile ahead by the time they reached the Bluestem boundary.

5

The town's pariah dogs were sniffing and scuttling along the main street towards the ox-wagon camp – a ripe area that always produced life-sustaining scraps. A drunk crawled from between the props of a cabin, attempted to stand and kick a particularly probing tyke, fell over and silently retched. White Mesa was coming to life, but from the Todo Mercantile, Preston Mower wasn't noticing too much happening. He laid his razor aside and dressed quickly, and took a drink from the water jar on a table in a corner of the room that caught any light breeze.

He left the store, walked down the boardwalk towards the Bello Hotel. He paused a moment at the hitch-rail, looked at the brands on the two horses tied there, but nothing made an impression. He pushed through the batwings and made his way up to the bar, waited for the bartender who was with a group of men who were finishing off an all-night session at their table.

Leaning casually on the bar, he watched two men who looked like punchers. They were both sound asleep, sitting in the far corner. They had local news-sheets over their faces, beneath which they snorted with an easy rhythm.

'Those two are either real tired or real safe,' he suggested to the barkeep.

'I'd say real drunk,' the man replied. 'An' I'd be the one

to know.'

'Yeah, I guess. Is Foote up yet?'

'Ain't seen him. Go on up. You know where he is.' The barkeep returned to the game, pausing to shake his head as he watched Mower walk up the stairs. Moments later a door slammed above them and the players called for a last round of drinks.

Once inside Turner Foote's room, Mower stood with his back against the door. He looked on with a degree of loathing when the sheriff rolled over and blinked, stared at him with watery eyes.

'What time is it?' Foote asked.

'Between midnight an' noon. Is that near enough for you?' Mower regarded Foote sourly. 'I went out to see Ogden last night.'

'Tell me later.' Foote turned away and Mower took a step forward. With an angry pull he heaved a single bedcover from the bed.

'I'll tell you now, goddamnit. Get up.' Mower went to the window and sat down on the sill, waiting for Foote to rub the sleep from his eyes. The sheriff stood beside his bed, in his unflapped long-johns, looking for all the world like a plucked turkey.

'Did you know Ogden bought out Far Creek yesterday?' Mower demanded.

Foote didn't answer, sluiced his face briefly at the washstand, and dried himself on a tattered towel.

'Yeah, 'course you did,' Mower said dourly. 'You've more'n likely been celebratin' for the goddamn Bolas.' The merchant's voice rose as Foote turned to look at him. 'Well, perhaps you should start to mourn the event.'

'What the hell are you talkin' about, Mower?'

'Ogden told me he bought the oufit with his own money.'

Foote didn't react the way Mower expected. He went to the mirror and had a good look at his tongue. 'Nagh, he can't do that. He's got no authority,' he said, apparently unperturbed.

'That's 'cause we didn't think he'd need any. Now he's on to the Bluestem spread, doin' the same thing.'

'We'll take our share, whichever way he thinks he's cut it,' Foote suggested patiently. He pulled on his clothes, adjusted his badge of office and lifted his gun belt from the bed head. 'Bruno Ogden ain't Bolas. It only looks an' sounds like it.'

'You're some smart piece o' work, Foote, you know that,' Mower said. 'Go find Marge an' bring her to the store, lickety-split.' The man gave him a look of derision, then without another word, he pulled open the door, hurried down the stairs and left the hotel.

The heat waves rolled down the main street, but for Preston Mower the morning was cooling fast as he bolted raisin biscuits and beans in a grub house opposite his mercantile. From where he sat at the end of the counter he watched Turner Foote walk from the main street towards where Marge Highgate lived. He gave him ten minutes, then returned to the store, entering by a side door that he didn't fully close.

He sat in his darkened office until he heard their voices, then stepped out to meet them. 'Come in, both o' you,' he said. 'Take chairs, this'll likely take a while.'

'That's what the sheriff's just told me.' Marge Highgate was pale, her greying hair drawn into a tight bun, lifting the corners of her eyes. Waiting for Mower to explain, she slapped irritatedly at Foote's hand as it touched her shoulder.

For the shortest time, Mower wondered if there was any-

36

thing between the two. 'Ogden's settin' out to get Bluestem. Did the good sheriff tell you that?' he murmured.

'You're a fool, Mower,' Marge replied coolly. 'Now, are you going to tell us what Ogden said, or do I have to ride to Bolas to find out?'

The trader eyed the lady, chewed his bottom lip for a moment. 'Ogden bought Far Creek with his own money,' he started intently. 'He's no intention of throwin' it in with his Bolas pool. Kind o' weaken the bloodline.'

Marge let her eyes close, as though in thought. She took a deep breath, waiting for Mower to continue.

'He knows if *we* can rope in Bluestem, *he'll* be the big augur. Not one coffee bean will roll through Hog Flats without his say so. If dollars won't swing it, he'll use the power of a gun.'

Now Marge looked directly into Mower's eyes. She read the submissive intent, but controlled her disdain. 'I saw Mollie Broad in town yesterday. What did she want?' she asked. 'I'm guessing she didn't come to sell.'

'Huh, what do any of 'em want? Time. She wanted time to settle up.'

'How much does she owe you?'

'I don't know. Not a fortune,' the trader rasped. 'Does it matter? Bluestem's down an' out.'

'But *we're* not on the way *up*,' Marge snapped back. 'Hell, I wonder why I chose half-bakes like you two. I'll have to whup Ogden on my own. The next time Bluestem brings a wagon to town, let them have their supplies.'

'Yeah sure, an' who pays?' Mower leaned forward, his big pasty features real close to Marge. 'You think I'm goin' bankrupt to advance you an' your own plans?'

'Just give them what they want,' Marge repeated and stood up. 'You have no choice. Either look like you're grubstaking Bluestem, or lose your investment in Bolas. You understand?'

Mower shifted his feet with unease and confusion. Acutely aware of being dismissed and of Foote's silent sneer, he moved back a step.

'There's only been a couple of things in my life I've really wanted,' Marge continued. 'Bluestem should have been one of them. Would have been if. . . .'

'If a big freight outfit hadn't decided to camp alongside the creek, an' if Elmer Broad hadn't met someone else.' Mower angrily supplied a finish to what Marge had started to say.

Marge decisively lifted a half-full tin mug of stale coffee from Mower's work desk, and without expression, she hurled the contents up and across Mower's front. 'Give them what they want,' she said coolly. 'Trick me, and I'll see you get stuck like the pig you rightly are.'

Mower had an uneasy recall of the two men he'd sent out to Bluestem. He'd done it in a turn of bluster knowing that Mollie Broad couldn't even offer them a good breakfast. He considered mentioning it, but Marge's hard-nosed stance was disturbing.

'Mal Deavis killed Redbone, yesterday,' he offered instead. 'He was scouting the Cholla.'

There was a heavy ensuing silence, and Marge carefully replaced the empty mug on the desk, gave both men a questioning look and walked towards the door. She stood in thought for a moment, and her voice was neutral. 'We all know what to do now,' she said.

The office door clunked shut behind her, the two men standing thoughtfully quiet until the store's front door also closed.

'Wheew. You get grasshoppers, prairie fires an' drought, then Marge Highgate comes sashayin' along, eh Pres?'

Mower was at a loss as to what reaction to give, even what to say. He slumped into a chair and leaned back, his chin sunken against his wet shirt front. 'Why don't you go to hell,' he muttered.

'Not quite time,' the sheriff snorted derisively. 'But I'm probably on the way,' he added, and followed on after Marge.

Mower looked around his empty office, his glance settling on some of the papers that had been dirtied by the coffee. Among them were bills for the Bluestem spread, and with a violent gesture he swept them to the floor, cursing his predicament and most everyone else he could think of.

6

The leaves of the big cottonwood that sheltered the ranch house were dry and wilted. It was mid-afternoon, most of the heat was burnt out of the day, and the lack of a breeze that brought only dust was a good thing. Will and Latch had spent eight hours riding line on Bluestem's boundary. Bolas gunhands had given up their pursuit when the two men approached the security of the home yard.

Ben Shoeville and Henri had ridden their shift, and now Will could see the crowns of their colourless range hats as they returned along the dry wash. He was resting with his back against a veranda upright. In the tired stillness he fixed his attention on a distant cloud. If rain came now, fell for long enough it could still save Bluestem. He knew of the desert's lust for life, its unique capacity to flower and die. If the moisture could be held, Hog Flats could provide once again. When the ranch house door opened he caught the drifted aroma of soap and Mollie Broad. 'So, how do we, you, us, get a few hundred head of beef to market?' he asked, starting on his train of thought.

Mollie sat down on the top step and looked openly at the new hands. 'Depends. If it was Bolas I'd be shipping to Whiterod. There's big new yards up there.'

'Yeah, except Ogden can't drive to Whiterod. Condor

Pass would be too much for any herd. We're talking cows, not pronghorns.' Will rolled his body forwards, stepped down to the hard ground. 'Besides, the beef that's boxed in is Bluestem, and the only way out's towards White Mesa.'

Mollie screwed up her face, narrowed her eyes as she looked at Will. 'Preston Mower always handled the buying from this valley. Most shipments went to the army buyer at Tyler's Post, the rest to Sweetwater.'

A look of dawning appeared on Will's face. 'Yeah. Anywhere but south,' he said.

'What does that mean? What are you thinking?' Mollie asked.

'I'm thinking Mower's got an eye for a chance like a turkey buzzard has for a turkey with a limp. Him *and* Ogden. Perhaps the Apache were right all along. Land belongs to nobody. When this drought breaks there'll be grass enough for everyone. Where will Ogden and his Bolas be then?'

'Still here? Won't they be the *everyone*, by then?' Latch suggested tentatively, avoiding the eye of Mollie or Will.

Along the blistering road from the creek, Shoeville and Henri bobbed and shimmered almost as optical illusions, dissolving, re-emerging as horse riders as they entered the yard. They dismounted, pushed their mounts into the gloom of the barn before walking to the group gathered around the veranda steps.

The silence was charged as they all took it in turns to look at one another. 'I reckon there's some bad medicine headed this way,' Shoeville said, breaking the suspense.

'Yes. Maybe it would be better if Miss Mollie stayed in town,' Henri put in.

Will bent down and picked up a handful of warm dirt, kept his face averted as he let it fall through his fingers.

'We certainly ain't headed for a clambake . . . a rehearsal for Thanksgiving,' he added.

Mollie turned towards Shoeville, looked for something to read in his face. 'I can hear you all out. But don't forget whose ranch this still is, Ben,' she said.

Shoeville spat out the pebble he was rolling around his mouth. 'If . . . *when* shooting starts, we don't want you here. Of course we don't. That's the nub of it.'

'Will says there's Bluestem beef up there.' Mollie's head moved in the direction of the pass. 'That means there's others . . . elsewhere.'

Shoeville levelled a positive gaze at her. 'Then we go get 'em. Chowse 'em back into the valley.' He then looked towards Will and Latch for their approval.

'Or arrange for the law to get it done,' Will offered instead.

Henri grimaced. 'Turner Foote's not in the cattle business,' he said, resenting the thought.

'Did you see him as you rode through town?' Mollie asked of Will.

'No ma'am. Only Mower and a few people along the creek.'

'Goddamn creeks'll be the death of me,' Mollie murmured wryly. 'Well right now, Foote's the weak link . . . like a rotten door hinge.' She stood up and shook the dust from her clothes. 'Ben, have you figured what we're all going to do?'

Shoeville had a shell belt hanging from one shoulder. His face was damp and strained, his eyes almost shut against the brassy glare. 'If it's Bluestem, it's ours. There's not much more to say.'

'Tell it to the law first, Ben.' There was an uneasy silence between the two men, then Will continued. 'That's what the law's meant to be there for. If it doesn't work, then we'll do it Ogden's way.'

'I'd like to override half o' that idea,' Shoeville said.

'I know you would.' Will's face was impassive. 'But longer term, you want the law behind *you*, not riding shotgun for Bolas.'

'OK, we'll try it civil and legal like,' Shoeville said glumly. 'But only until the very second it don't work.'

Latch looked at Will and winked. 'Gives a new meanin' to "livin' for the moment",' he agreed. 'Me an' Henri can stay here an' take care o' things . . . in case some of 'em pay us a visit.'

'While me an' Ben mosey on into town,' Will said.

Mollie nodded her understanding of their decision. She watched them walk into the barn, then without another word, turned and re-entered her ranch house.

'Pack horse'll come in real handy,' Will said, picking up a halter and blanket. 'We'll take it . . . pick up supplies at the mercantile.'

'Todo? Mower? Hell, great idea,' Shoeville almost spat his keenness. 'But he's still goin' to demand payment.'

Will gave a thin smile. 'It don't look like it, but I'm wearing a few hundred dollars. Me and Latch will be only too pleased to throw in with the Bluestem pot. We'll regard it as an investment.'

Shoeville studied Will through the gloom of the barn. 'You sure don't look like no meal ticket,' he growled.

'My pa said never to judge a man by the coat he wears.' Will jerked the cinches before mounting his horse. 'Before we came here, we ran some of our own broncs into the remuda at Tyler's Post,' he explained. 'The agent there's paying twenty-five for beef.' Will half turned in the saddle, held out the lead rope of the pack horse. 'So, we should be able to pull Bluestem from the chughole, don't you reckon?'

'Yep. All we've got to do's get there,' Shoeville grinned. 'But it's a good idea ... generous to a fault,' he said, and rode into the bright, dusty heat.

Mower saw them coming. He recognized Will Chalk, shuddered with the anticipation of trouble. He pulled his chair back into the deeper shade of the store, settled down to wait.

Will and Ben Shoeville nodded good-humouredly as they rode carefully through a band of interested youngsters. They continued down the street to the Bello Hotel, tied their horses and went inside.

Mower moved outside the mercantile, and leaning against a veranda post, pondered on the optimism of the riders' pack mule. Then a slight smile lifted one corner of his mouth. Ben Shoeville was faithful Bluestem, no doubt in town to try again for an essential supply. He thought wryly about Marge Highgate's directive, went back inside to wait for the trade. He had little doubt Shoeville would be thunderstruck when an even more desperate request for credit was granted.

From the Bello Hotel, Turner Foote first saw the Bluestem men in the backbar mirror. He turned to face them, conscious of the small beads of sweat on his upper lip.

'Shoeville,' he acknowledged. 'Who's the stranger?' he added as the pair walked up to him.

'New hand. His name's Chalk, but he does speak for himself.' Shoeville motioned to the barkeep. 'Two beers.'

'Hiring, eh? Hmm, I thought Bluestem had gone out o' business.' The sheriff stretched out a hand and picked up his glass, drank while his words sunk in.

Shoeville looked to Will, then back to Foote. 'Hell no. We aim to get bigger,' he replied. 'In fact, you can help us

. . . one o' the reasons we're here, Sheriff.'

The barkeep laid change on the bar and stood back. He'd seen something in Ben Shoeville's eyes that worried him and he backed off further. Most men in his trade kept a shotgun under the counter for protection. He kept that, together with an old storm cellar door he could pull up as a shield against firearms trouble.

'Some of us have been out for a good look around. For one reason or another, poked into places we wouldn't normally have rhyme or reason to,' Shoeville continued. 'Up in the pass, along the Cholla, we discovered a few hundred head of Bluestem beef. They're all boxed in with good grass an' plenty o' water. We aim to run 'em down the line to Tyler's Post if the weather breaks.'

'That's a lot o' beef. All Bluestem, you say,' Foote spluttered into his glass. 'At a decent price, it could sure help out the Broad girl.'

'Could help us all out, Sheriff. Trouble is, it's all on Bolas land, an' under guard.'

Foote attempted to calm himself, edge away from fear and confusion. 'Assumin' they ain't all legitimate strays, what would Bolas want or be doin' with that quantity of Bluestem stock? Hell, they must be hard put to water their own?'

'Looks to me like the Bruno Ogden Land and Stock Company ain't hard put for anything, Sheriff.' Will's voice was just above a hoarse whisper. 'They're doing just fine. Of course, they had to make a barrier across the Cholla and divert the creekwater to make it so. As of the moment, Ogden's made this side of Condor Pass drier than a goddamn tobacco box.'

Foote waved his empty beer glass. 'Sounds to me like a case o' the heat makin' mad dogs out o' sane men.'

'I don't know who or what the hell you're talkin' about,

but I know that greedy men never know when they've had enough,' Shoeville rasped in reply.

Foote didn't bother to continue. He looked in the direction of the barkeep. 'Fill us up again, *amigo*,' he said.

The pull of futility showed on Will's face, his grinding jaw. 'We just told you. There's Bluestone stock being held in a box canyon. Least you can do is take your sheriff's badge up there for a look,' he insisted.

Foote's returning glare showed both irritation and concern. 'You got a lot o' nose, feller. What would the Bolas company want with Mollie Broad's wayward stock?' He shook his head. 'An' no stranger's goin' to wheedle me into a gimcrack range war.'

'Stranger or not, I've seen what I've seen,' Will pushed.

'Bluestem beef that's fit to muster will be rattlebone by now,' the sheriff said.

Shoeville grasped Foote by the shoulder and turned him face to face. 'They're fat-to-the-ground Bluestem stock, an' we're Bluestem riders. You're sayin' you want us to sort it out *our* way?'

The lawman looked to where Shoeville had grabbed him, took a slow step back. 'Your way ain't to go around makin' wild charges. Bruno Ogden's as honest as the next man. So's the way his company operates.'

'Once maybe. Now he's a cow-thief. A rustler wearin' store-boughts.'

Fear now touched at Sheriff Foote. 'I don't know what you two are fixin' to do, but if it's carvin' beef from Bolas grass, I'd advise against.'

'If that *is* what we're doin', Sheriff, there's nothing you can say that changes my mind. Nothin'!' Shoeville banged his glass down on the bar. 'Let's go, Will,' he rasped. 'We've provisions to get.'

Foote lost control of his temper. He stepped in front of

the two men and held up a restraining hand. 'Move one cow on to Bluestem, an' you'll lose it ... maybe more. That's a lawful warnin'.'

Shoeville cursed, balled both fists. 'Goddamnit, you're not telling me to kiss our own beef farewell. Throw your weight around with mescal drunks and tinhorns, Sheriff, but don't threaten me with your divisive law.'

Foote wiped the back of his hand across his mouth. His eyes were shifty and vicious. 'You're beat, Shoeville, so I'll take your words. An' you'll have the girl use you as bait. When you're all dead she'll still be alive. There's no future in Hog Flats. Not if you buck Ogden.'

'I've always been the hopeful traveller, Sheriff, an' I'm not dead yet.' Shoeville followed Will to the door, stood for a moment, his angry eyes taking in the uncertain figure of the lawman. 'Before I'm through, there'll be others with grass wavin' over 'em,' he warned.

Preston Mower was waiting for them. There was speculation in his cunning eyes, and he wondered if the new Bluestem hand worked on a grudge. If Will was trouble, he knew it rarely came single-handed.

'What can I do for you fellers?' he asked.

'Fill this order,' Shoeville said with little regard for civility.

The trader held out his hand and took the list that Mollie Broad had brought in two days earlier. He looked over Shoeville's shoulder to the baking street, saw Sheriff Foote standing under a drooping cottonwood diagonally across the main street.

There was impending danger in the men's stance and Mower decided to take a side-step and to hell with Marge Highgate. 'Are you considering a cash payment?' he enquired with a slick smile.

47

In response, Will pulled some bills from his pocket and handed them over. 'We won't be asking for a markdown . . . not just yet,' he said.

Mower managed to steady himself from the rising antagonism. 'I'd like to forget what happened the other day,' he said, laying the money on the counter. 'I can back whoever I want. We live too close to be scatterin' manure on each other's pastures . . . so to speak.'

'Well, you don't want to go supporting the flame that fans the fire,' Will replied acidly. 'I reckon a man in your position's got a lot to lose . . . so to speak.'

'We don't want or need your support, Mower. Just the supplies we came in for,' Shoeville added.

Mower turned his pasty features to Will. 'Someone's got to give you some advice, cowboy,' he said. 'You ought to get from these parts . . . quick. You're the kind who gets a clock tickin'.'

Will nodded thoughtfully. 'And add a good skinning knife to the order,' he answered.

7

The range was like carpet pile, ruffled by the relentless blue norther. The sky was coppery, thunderheads building over the distant San Andreas Mountains. To the west and north, rangeland was cut by deep gullies, low eroded rimrock. From atop one of these, Bruno Ogden could make out the irregular shapes and outbuildings of Bluestem ranch.

'We might have more to worry about than cows,' he said as he pushed his horse through the loops of rock, keeping to the vantage points. He looked over his shoulder, saw the glance between Mal Deavis and Copper John, and reined in.

'I don't think so,' Deavis answered as he rode up. 'Right now she's crazy enough to fight all the law officers east an' west o' the Rio Grande.'

They heard, but didn't see the approaching rider until his crumpled stovepipe hat showed above the dry wash. The comanchero, Pito, came up to the rim, wiped his face in his hands and glanced at the Bolas riders.

'Shoeville an' new feller are in White Mesa. The Frenchman an' *viejo* are with the girl at the ranch,' he said.

For the moment Ogden ignored Pito, pulling his horse around to glare impatiently at Deavis. 'I hope you told the crew to move that beef. If those two sons-of-bitches from Bluestem decide to ride the box canyon again, I want it empty . . . the beef pushed through the canyon.'

'That's what we've been up here for,' Deavis replied, abrupt and hard-nosed.

'And now I'm going to talk to the Broad girl.' Ogden put his fine sorrel to the slope and fiddle-footed down to the dry wash. The others were lined out behind him, but a mile further on they closed up.

'They say the Frenchman's defensive . . . unpredictable,' Deavis exclaimed. 'He could blow someone's head off.'

'I don't think so. Be a tough shot for someone who's not a natural gunsman.' Ogden pulled a large white bandana up over his nose, settled himself for the ride. In the clear desert air and in the failing light, distance was a deceptive thing to measure. From the rising peaks of Condor Pass it hadn't looked far, but it was first dark when they rode on to the back pasture of Bluestem's home ground. They rode around the small graveyard with its homespun markers. The names were wind and sand-scoured now, but one was clearer than the others. Ogden leaned forward, squinted at the carved letters. ELMER BROAD. NOW RESTING PEACEFUL.

Ogden sat straight in the saddle, peered into the shadows ahead. 'Stay out of sight and wait for me,' he said and rode on alone.

'We got company,' Latchford Loke reached for the rifle that was propped against the wall. He looked around, sweeping the fall-off into the creek, searching for other riders. He heard a horse whicker, and he levered up a shell, and called out.

'You're on Bluestem property. State your business.'

'Name's Ogden. Bruno Ogden of the Bolas. I'm here to

talk with Mollie Broad.'

Latch released the hammer of the rifle. 'We'll see if she wants to talk with you. Stay where you are.'

'I'll talk,' Mollie said as she came out of the house.

Ogden heeled his sorrel forward. 'Tell your man to point his rifle somewhere's else,' he murmured.

Holding a double-barrelled shotgun, Henri walked from the bunkhouse. Latch waited until he had taken position at the near corner of the house.

Mollie looked at both men, nodded and they slowly lowered their guns. 'I'm assuming you haven't come to kill me, Mr Ogden,' she called out. 'But if I were you, I'd keep my hands empty and clear in the open.'

Ogden gave a tight smile and held up the palms of both hands, knee'd his horse closer to the veranda. 'This is a friendly visit, ma'am. The last time I looked, I wasn't armed,' he said, curling his fingers around the saddlehorn. 'And it's been a long time since I said *that* to anyone.'

Mollie almost returned the smile. 'It's a long way back to your business, and the day's starting to wane. So just say what's on your mind.' Mollie's eyes glittered fiercely in the fading light. Within a deep fold of her calico dress, her right hand clutched the bone handle of a small-bore pistol.

'I heard you're hiring gunhands, Miss Broad.' Ogden kept his irritation in check, his glance ignoring Latch and Henri. 'Two of them crossed the boundary and shot up one of my line camps.'

'It's a tad early for bedtime stories, Ogden. And if your sources were reliable, you'd know I haven't a plugged nickel to hire gunhands with. Fact is, you're holding Bluestem stock on your range and we're coming after it.' With that, Mollie did return a stiff smile.

Ogden shrugged. 'If you believe that, why not send over

51

a rider or two tomorrow and check it out?' he said, noticing Latch who walked quickly across the porch and into the house.

Henri looked across his shoulder when the heavy door squeaked on its hinges. Nervy and uncertain of what was happening, he lifted his shotgun and fired with Ogden nearly in his sights. Next moment, the crash of another gun blasted out from close behind him. He felt a great pulse of air, a hammer blow to the back of his head and he shot forward, down to the warm, choking dust.

On impulse, Mollie brought up her own Colt and fired. The way she'd been taught, happened, and she pulled the trigger again, then again. Ogden cursed, jerked sideways, kicking his sorrel into the yard. 'Treacherous wild bunch,' his voice cracked out.

Latch backed away from the door as the explosions reverberated and flashed against the darkening ranch house. He stopped, took a step forward as Mollie ran into the front parlour. 'Get in here,' he yelled. He grabbed her by the arm, pulled her flat against the back wall.

A breeze blew in and a chair scraped across the floorboards. Latch saw the steely, glinting line of a rifle barrel as a figure came through an open doorway into the room. He stood very still and quiet, waited until the intruder was almost in front of him and Mollie. Then he elbowed himself away from the wall.

'Henri wouldn't come in the back way,' he grated, and lit the room with the flashes and firing of his carbine. He swung violently, nearly blinded, as a bullet smashed his shoulder, flung him back against Mollie and the wall. Desperately, single-handed, he fired once again. This time he saw the intruder's face, but momentarily, as the bullet hit the man between coal-black eyes. Then he cursed again, louder, as he realized there were two men, not one.

He heard, rather than saw the other man running for the back door. Now Mollie was turning to fire. She fired three more times, then the hammer fell on an empty case. It was a shadowy figure she was firing at. The man staggered sideways, falling heavily against the door frame of the back door before disappearing into the outside gloom. The sounds echoed through the house, rooms filling with acrid cordite. With their hearts pounding, Latch and Mollie stood and watched. Shocked and silent, they listened to the thumping of hoofs on hard-packed dirt as a rider galloped across and away from the home yard.

'Light one o' your lamps,' Latch said. Moments later he was holding himself against the wall, staring down at the body that was bathed in the yellow glow.

'They must've been after you, ma'am. To come into the house like that,' he said in a voice devoid of emotion.

'Who is he?' Mollie asked.

'I don't know. I'd probably recognize him if he'd got a face. It's me I'm worried about.'

Mollie put the lamp down and helped Latch to the couch. 'Sit here. Henri's been hit too.'

Latch was dazed. His shoulder hurt bad and the fingers of his left arm were numbing up. When Mollie returned a few minutes later, she was deeply anxious. 'I can't move Henri,' she said sadly. 'He's too heavy.' She looked closely at Latch's wound, gritted her teeth and felt the back of his shoulder. 'The bullet's gone clean through. It's the flesh ... the muscle that hurts. At least I won't have to attempt any surgery,' she added with a wan smile. 'I'll go and heat some water, something to clean up with.'

'Can you load my rifle afore you do that?' Latch asked. When Mollie had gone, he got to his feet and walked to the front door of the parlour. *If he's that bad, moving him might kill him*, he thought, looking across to where Henri was lying. *Tend to the living, I say.* He turned his back to the home yard, took another look at the dead man on the floor of the parlour. 'Reckon more got away than stayed,' he called out to Mollie. Then he cursed, faltered to the couch when his senses whirled.

A distinct drumming of hoofs came out of the night as Will and Shoeville rode to the tethering rail of the Bluestem ranchhouse. Returning from town, the two men had heard the piercing crack of gunfire, now they smelled the remaining wisps of low-lying gunsmoke. Will took the veranda steps two at a time, kicked at the spent cartridge cases.

'Where the hell are they?' he rasped.

'Henri's over here. Could be hurt bad,' Shoeville exclaimed breathlessly from the yard.

Just inside the front door to the parlour, Will quartered the room with his Colt. 'Who the. . . ?' he started, seeing the body on the floor.

'I'm here, Will,' Latch said. 'Bullet wound ain't so bad, but I'll live . . . don't feel so chirpy though.'

'Was this Ogden? Where's Mollie?'

'We had a visit from him. He brought two of his gunnies.'

'Yeah. That one's a comanchero. Name o' Pito . . . I think. Looks like Ogden's decided to make an open fight of it. He must be desperate. Where's Mollie?'

'I'm here, Will,' Mollie gasped as she came into the room carrying a bowl of hot water. 'Thank God you're back . . . you and Ben. You can help me get Henri in here. Latch needs some cleaning and sewing.'

A half hour later, owing to shock and mescal, Henri was in a deep sleep on the couch. His was a bad graze wound, now cleansed and wadded with willow poultice, tied with strips of clean towel.

'And that leaves you, Mollie,' Will started. 'Ogden's not ended the affair, not by a long chalk. I reckon you should go into White Mesa. At least until this is over.'

Mollie stared back, her eyes glittering with righteous anger. 'This is my home. You think I'm letting a virtual stranger bid me to leave it?'

'It's common sense,' Latch said bluntly. 'I sure wouldn't stay here given a choice. Not for the next few days, anyhow.'

There was an uneasy silence. 'I wouldn't want to see you hurt, or worse. It's unnecessary,' Shoeville said, sounding like he was thinking aloud. 'If you feel so strong for Bluestem, why'd you want to put your life in danger?'

'And where would I go, Ben?' Mollie flushed gently as she considered the sense and feeling in Shoeville's voice, read the unspoken message in his eyes. 'The Bello Hotel?'

'No, ma'am.' Shoeville leaned forward, almost conspiratorial. 'It's pretty clear we're all ready to finish what Ogden started. But if any one of us gets caught considerin' your wellbein' or whereabouts, that's it. It don't take long to get shot. Put clear . . . you'll be in the way.'

'Thank you, Ben. That is very clear.' Mollie stepped between Will and Latch, went out on to the veranda. Summer lightning flashed restlessly over the mountains. Thunder followed, muttering around the rimrocked foothills, and a hunter's moon silvered Hog Flats.

Shoeville came out and stood beside Mollie. 'No reason why you can't turn in,' he suggested. 'We'll figure what to do in the mornin'.'

'Tell me what you've decided, you mean,' Mollie replied. 'I *could* stay with Marge Highgate,' she added, turning towards the front door. 'After all, we've a lot in common.'

'We've all got some o' *that*,' Shoeville said obliquely, letting her brush closely past him.

8

The following morning, Mollie drove her pie buggy to town. Ben Shoeville sat beside her, his horse strung out from the tailboard. They rattled across the rough-hewn bridge which spanned the creek, took the left fork.

'No matter what happens . . . what you hear, stay close to town,' Shoeville advised without taking his eyes off the trail.

'I will. But it's not going to be easy at Marge Highgate's place with all of you dodging Bolas . . . heaven knows what else out at Bluestem.' Clear concern was in every word of Mollie's voice.

'Well, we're not for the skedaddle. An' Ogden looks like he's wantin' to make it real personal.'

'So what are we going to do, Ben?' Mollie asked more fervently. 'The man's got himself a crew on fighting wages . . . more, I'll wager. Why not let the sheriff step in and handle it?'

'The sheriff? Turner Foote?' There was open contempt in Shoeville's voice. Mollie turned towards him, saw the darkness in his eyes.

'We'll make things so tough for Ogden's goddamn Land an' Stock Company, they'll be prayin' for another Apache uprisin'.' Shoeville leaned forward and jerked at the brake lever as they drew alongside the Highgate picket fence. He swung to the ground, ducked under the horse's head to the wagon's offside. Taking a fraction longer than necessary, he took Mollie's hand, assisted her to the ground as Marge Highgate came out on to her stoop.

'Hello Mollie. You come to visit?' The woman's voice sounded friendly.

'I've been evicted . . . run out of my own home by my own people,' Mollie replied calmly.

'I'm sure regretful of that, ma'am . . . the suddenness of it all,' Shoeville said, lifting a bulky travelling bag from the wagon. 'I'll take the rig on to the livery.'

'Is there something I'm missing, Ben?' Mollie asked thoughtfully. 'I know this is a lot more than a burr under your saddle, but you've got . . . unmanageable.'

Shoeville regarded Mollie for a moment. 'I owe Ogden for Lew Redbone, for last night, for Henri, for what he's doin' to you. It's a debt needs payin' back,' he said stubbornly.

'I said for you to see Sheriff Foote before you leave town, Ben. Look on it as a work order. You understand?'

'Yes ma'am,' Shoeville accepted. He climbed back on the seat, shook out the reins and drove off slowly.

'Let's get you out of this heat, Mollie. Come on inside,' Marge Highgate said with a quick glance at the withdrawing pie buggy. 'You're very welcome. I get lonesome,' she added, picking up the valise.

'Yes, I do too. I didn't realize how much.' Mollie was weary as she followed the older woman into the house.

'You can have the room along here. I'll show you.' Marge smiled.

The room was small, clean and comfortably furnished, cool after the hot winds of the Flats. Mollie stared blankly around her, then unpacked and hurried out into the kitchen.

*

'Now what is all this about, Mollie? Tell me.' As she spoke, Marge pointed to a tray on top of the oven. 'Four pies. Two meat, two fruit. I'm not sure why I made so much . . . must have known there was company,' she added with a smile.

'Sounds like you mean more than me.' Mollie didn't sound particularly interested. 'I'm sorry about this, Marge. Out of the blue . . . you know.'

'Nonsense. We don't live in a world of appointments, Mollie. Besides, we're almost kin aren't we? Good heavens, sometimes it seems like only yesterday your pa came to town.' Beneath Marge's geniality, she was recalling, pushing away an old bitter thought. *And he married someone else while I sat waiting . . . and hoping.* 'Still, that's enough of that. It's more comfortable in the parlour, and you can tell me what it is that's troubling you so.'

For ten minutes Mollie related her story, the recent events out at Bluestem. 'It's obvious there's going to be more trouble . . . final, bad trouble.' Mollie was near to choking with emotion.

'I've listened to every word you've said, Mollie. But I do have to get to the store,' Marge replied. 'It's where I wanted to go as you arrived. I won't be long. It is quite important.'

Mollie attempted a smile. 'With those comforting pies out there, the temptation's too great. Baking hasn't been top of my chores lately. Why not let *me* go? The walk's what I need right now, even in the heat.'

'No, no.' Madge lifted a sombrero from the hook behind the door. 'You've had enough for one day. Besides, it's another opportunity to bother Preston Mower.'

Mollie didn't have time to say that, if that was the case, their combined force would be first-rate, even pleasing.

For a moment, Marge halted at the front door. 'You can put the coffee on the hot-plate, Mollie,' she called before hurrying off to the main street.

Along the narrow boardwalk, Marge took advantage of meagre overhead shade. She approached Todo Mercantile, and went in at the front as Mower came out of the back office. The trader cursed silently and held the door open, stood with his back against it. Mollie glared around her, puffed her cheeks and bent back the front brim of her hat.

'Ben Shoeville's taking Foote out to Bolas,' she said.

'An' how'd you know that?' Mower scowled.

'Mollie Broad told me not more than a quarter hour ago. There was trouble out at her place last night and two of her men got hurt. But it cost Ogden. One of his venomous comancheros was killed and another badly wounded.'

'She rode into town to tell *you*?' Mower demanded impatiently.

'No. Ben Shoeville brought her to me for safe keeping.' Marge pulled the brim of her hat back down. 'Get word to Ogden. Tell him it looks like open stakes now. If you like, point out the ace is up *my* sleeve.'

A pang of doubt beset Mower and he frowned. 'You sure she doesn't suspect anything? You?'

'Huh, like sleeping with the enemy?' Marge moved towards the door. 'She suspects nothing. Look out for Shoeville when he leaves. And don't forget the message for Ogden.'

As Marge left the store, a wicked smile crooked Mower's face as he went to sit in his resting-watching chair. Not long after, Ben Shoeville walked from the livery with his horse. Mower saw the Bluestem ramrod tie up outside the sheriff's office, and he settled down to wait.

*

The sheriff's office was a big, sparely furnished room. Against the far wall, Turner Foote sat at his desk with his feet up, contemplating his next measure of whiskey.

'Get yourself settled furthest from the front door, and just keep quiet,' a venerable town mayor had advised him. 'They barge in, all bluster and up in arms, but get discouraged by the time they reach you and your desk.' It was a strategy Foote had seen work on more than one occasion.

Now, he didn't look up at Ben Shoeville's entrance, and the Bluestem man waited a moment silently watching him. When the lawman still didn't respond, Shoeville re-opened the door, fiercely kicked it shut with his heel.

It jolted Foote, made him push himself from his chair. He stood with suspicion and fear crimping his face.

'Swallow hard and grab your traps, Sheriff,' Shoeville said, taking a few steps forward. 'We've got some ridin' ahead of us.'

'Ridin' to where?' Foote asked hoarsely.

'Ogden attacked Bluestem ranch last night. They left a dead man behind. That's a sheriff's business.'

For many seconds, Foote stood silently thinking. He started to say something, but produced nothing, the impact of Shoeville's mission sinking in. 'I warned you an' that new Chalk feller what would happen if. . . .'

Shoeville interrupted with another step forward, no attempt to hide his anger. 'Just grab a hat. I'll get you ready myself if I have to.'

'I'm the sheriff, not one o' your saddlers, goddamnit,' Foote replied, crabbing along the rear wall of his office.

Shoeville yanked a range hat off the hook and threw it at the lawman. 'There's no witness, so I'll treat you any way I want, you son-of-a-bitch. Put that on. I'm not havin' the entrails o' your head burn up.'

Foote's slack face loosened even more with fear. He

61

stared at the door, shuddered when Shoeville opened it and gestured towards the street.

'I'm not goin' anywhere just yet. Not if it ain't in my territory.' Foote avoided Shoeville, turned more towards the Bello Hotel than the livery. 'I won't be forgettin this,' he rasped as Shoeville's tough fingers clamped around his forearm, twisting him around.

He stumbled back towards the livery, his nerves jumpy, his breathing short and panicky.

'You're not supposed to,' Shoeville told him.

The sheriff had become silent now. He led a big chestnut mare from its stall, lifted a blanket and saddle from the hooks on the wall and threw them across the back of the horse. He worked with piqued resolution, tightening cinches and jerking at straps. *A bit longer*, he thought. *Just a bit longer, and then to hell with the Broads.* Then he reflected on Shoeville's story. *After what happened last night, will Ogden cut loose when a Bluestem rider shows up . . . even if he is accompanied by the town sheriff?* He glanced across the seat of the saddle, saw that Shoeville had a wary eye on him and decided on an action to take.

Leading the horse out to the hot, dry street, Foote walked slowly to his office. He was gone for less than five minutes before re-appearing with a rifle and a box of shells. Once the gun was sheathed and the shells pocketed, he swung heavily into the saddle. He lifted the reins and glanced at the waiting Shoeville. 'Got more authority than a badge,' he replied to the unspoken question. 'An' this man who was killed? How'd it happen?'

'He was in Mollie Broad's parlour, an' not by invitation.'

'Did anyone get a name?'

'Pito . . . that's all.'

'You sure about that?'

'I'm sure he's dead. Let's get goin'.'

A crushing weakness ate at the sheriff's vitals as he knee'd his horse towards the creek bridge. He shivered, although sweat was already trickling freely between his shoulder blades. Everything about Shoeville's implacable demeanour was trouble. There was no solace in knowing that Bruno Ogden would be looking for an appropriate amount of damage.

9

A dry, dusty wind blew off the Flats. Between the blusters, the small smudge that was the Bluestem ranch range appeared to float in the coloured air that clouded the pass the two men had to ride through.

'We can ride at sundown.' Turner Foote half turned to look at Shoeville, read the grim resentment in the man's face and swore angrily. 'Hell, why not?'

'Just keep your mouth shut,' Shoeville muttered. He'd been thinking of the rifle in Foote's saddle scabbard, wondered if the lawman carried a hide-out gun on him somewhere.

'I just want to know.' Foote hauled up his horse. 'If we'd sent word to Ogden, he'd have rode into town. There'd be no need o' this, goddamnit.'

Shoeville gave the swiftest of thoughts to the man's gripe, almost considerate. 'There's a plaque hangin' inside your office door says somethin' about justice an' your own doorstep. You forgot that, Sheriff? An' you're bein' paid.'

Foote didn't answer. He was too engaged with thoughts about Ogden, what the man would do, or get done, when they rode through the pass. For the umpteenth time he considered his options, even thought about the irony of carrying guns.

Gradually, the two riders worked their way towards the mountains, suffering weariness from the heat and gruelling trail.

'For Chris'sake's, Shoeville,' Foote began after a long period of silence. 'You know that if we carry through with this, there's a lot o' people gettin' hurt. Why should you side with a barleycorn outfit like Bluestem? Hog Flats is ruined for cattle, and it'll take more'n a couple of cloudbursts to soften the land. Why pick on Bruno Ogden for a fight?'

Having harboured similar thoughts, even uncertainties, for some time, Shoeville considered the man's words. 'I'll make it simple,' he said. 'He's a harmful bully an' needs to be put down.'

'An' *you'll* come out of it with ten years of breakin' rocks on the Tularosa Turnpike.'

'Not with you as a respectable witness, I won't.' Shoeville leaned from the saddle and smacked the haunch of Foote's big mare. 'Get goin', star-toter.'

The sheriff was still riven with nerves as they rode through the pass. The day's early alcohol was rising from his gut, but didn't account for the sickness he felt on seeing movement high up in the canyon walls. By now, Ogden's guards would have sent word back to the ranch house. Foote prayed there'd be no shooting before he'd had time to speak his part.

Standing under the broad overhang of his portico, Bruno Ogden leaned against a white painted upright as he watched Shoeville and Foote enter the home yard. His face was taut, but his eyes bright and sharp.

'Come on in, Sheriff,' he called out. 'You've been a long time in getting here.'

Foote lifted a weary leg over the cantle and swung to the

ground, sat stiffly down on the steps. 'Goddamnit, these ain't the conditions for a man to be out ridin'.'

'Sorry, I don't remember extending an invite.' Ogden's tone was disdainful, hardening as it settled on Shoeville. 'And you're a ways from home, cowpoke.'

Shoeville looked around him. He knew that anyone who'd got themselves into Ogden's position wouldn't be taking any chances. He noted the low-lying ranch house, the green grass and arching willows, the glint of lowering sunshine on the windows. Off to the west, up-canyon, he saw rising curls of dust. They were most likely extra guards setting out to seal off Bolas.

'Don't worry about me. I'm just taggin' along with the law,' Shoeville said. He read the hostility in Ogden's manner, considered that if acknowledging White Mesa and Territorial law, disrespect and antagonism were mutual.

'So what is it you rode out to tell me, Sheriff?' Ogden asked.

'It's about a fair size herd o' Bluestem beef up in the hills.'

Ogden stepped down off the porch, kneeled close to Foote. 'There's a few who say I'm foolish over some things. But never about cattle. You ought to know that, Turner.' He looked again at Shoeville, this time more doubtfully. 'And that's why you're here.'

Shoeville was alert to the Bolas gunmen who were out in the shade of the trees. 'I don't think you're any kind of fool, Ogden. I think you're dishonest at best . . . wouldn't like to consider your worst,' he replied. If no one was going to mention the gun fight at Bluestem, he wasn't either. After all, Bolas had come off worse in that encounter . . . why continue the whys and wherefores? 'When you suckered Far Creek into a sale, you didn't consider the scrub beef . . . Bluestem mavericks roaming the higher ground.

66

Or did you?'

Ogden smiled. Aping a play pistol, he pointed two fingers at Shoeville's stomach. He thought about the ramrod's words, then looked up, his features set hard again. 'There's been no tally yet. When there is one, I'll let you know the mix.'

'Why not invite us in to help?' Shoeville suggested. 'It makes sense more and it's more neighbourly.'

'I don't do neighbourly. Hadn't you noticed?' Ogden snapped, triggering his forefinger.

'Hell, Bruno.' Foote's voice was chafed with uncertainty. 'Are you aimin' to move herds through the pass?'

'Not all of them, no. I've got a gather in a box canyon. I'm bringing them south of Condor Pass before they starve on Bluestem's dirt.'

'I've three riders I can throw into the cow hunt,' Shoeville felt a way in, a draw of anticipation. 'It'll make less work for you if we tally in the canyon.'

'Three riders, you say? I'll not have any strangers riding herd on stock that's belonging to me.'

'They won't be. I can guarantee it,' Shoeville said easily, almost laughing at the irony. 'They're trustworthy but hard, not soft waddies like most of us. Besides, from what I've seen so far, not all *your* riders are exactly kin.'

Ogden's face turned blank in spite of his tight smile. He stood up, glanced around the home ground as if confirming his security, looked at Foote, saw the discomfiture fleetingly play across the lawman's face.

'This is Bolas, Shoeville,' he said. 'An outfit that's worked hard to get what it wants. Right now, it's looking down on a stack of land and lodgings it means to own.'

'And you're powerful enough to get it?'

'Well, that's what we're going to find out.' Ogden's voice was flat, straightforward. 'I'm not setting to rile every

67

cowman in Hog Flats. I think you're probably a good man, but that's not a quality we use in business, is it?'

'I wouldn't say it was an exclusive. Go on.'

'The desert and drought has cut Bluestem back to nothing. Too few cows, too few hands, too little money. Lump it all together and what have you got? A busted hand, I'd say.' Ogden stared at Foote, bringing him into the conversation. 'There's an Act states, such property goes back to commissioners. Eh, Sheriff?'

The lawman nodded uncertainly. 'Ain't my specialty, but yeah, it's somethin' like that. If no one takes over.'

Shoeville was grinding his jaw with helpless irritation, but before he could say anything, Mal Deavis appeared from a side annexe of the ranch house. The gunman held his hands loosely at his sides, looked enquiringly towards Ogden. But the Bolas chief was watching anger cloud the Bluestem ramrod's face.

'You're down to legal tomfoolery, Ogden,' Shoeville said, watching Deavis as he spoke. He was weighing his chances, same time keeping his right hand well away from his own Colt. He lifted his left hand pointedly at the sheriff. 'I brought you here to explain how Bluestem stands. Tell him.'

'I'm a town sheriff, not a state legislator,' Foote retorted.

'Tell him he doesn't own the water rights across Hog Flats. That's got to be town sheriff stuff, goddamnit.'

'I know nothin' about water or its rights. Wherever it is,' Foote blazed, getting to his feet.

'You know that no one alters the course of a river or creek, unless you're a goddamn broody beaver,' Shoeville answered back. 'That water's here for all, including the Cholla. And right now, that's bone dry.'

'Are you telling us something we don't know?' Ogden asked.

'No. You know all right. You built a dam to run water down this side of Condor Pass.'

'A dam?' Ogden sounded incredulous. 'You've seen this?'

'Will Chalk has. He's not a man for imaginings or exaggeration.'

Ogden's eyes narrowed. 'I remember telling you to keep your men off Bolas,' he said. 'Now I'll tell you again, Shoeville. Stay off my range. Tell Chalk – anyone – that if I catch 'em this side of the Bluestem markers, I'll shoot them dead as trespassers, land scalpers, squatters, whatever. And with the law's blessing.'

'Huh, you mean backshot by one of your hired gunmen? Like they did for Lew Redbone?' Shoeville accused. 'Answer for the dam,' he persisted angrily. 'Look around at the greenness. How the hell can Bolas run herds and feed them when the rest of the valley's dying? How the hell does water manage to flow your way and not ours? Are you in touch with someone up above, perhaps an agreement with the law? You want to explain, Ogden?' Shoeville's contempt broke over the sheriff, who stood uneasy and ineffective.

'Hey. Did you get me to ride up here to get trapped . . . implicated in your goddamn scrap?' Foote blustered.

'Yeah, sort of,' Shoeville said, as though he wasn't sure any longer.

Ogden disregarded Foote. 'How about them beavers you mentioned?' he said through the slightest of smirks.

'They're smart, but they stop short at rolling rocks around,' Shoeville replied. 'Don't try and finagle me, boss man. And tell that carrion Deavis to crawl back into his daytime hole. If he makes any move for that gun of his while we're standing here, I'm getting at least one bullet into *you*. There's no significant law to worry about.'

'I'll look into this dam business.' Ogden turned away from Shoeville, stared thoughtfully at Foote as he spoke. 'You'd better head back to town,' he said. 'Apologize to that lonesome jug of corn.'

'At least you know where you are with a drink,' Foote murmured. 'I had no choice ... don't rightly know what I'm supposed to do. You'd better come up with somethin' soon.'

Ogden walked up the ranch-house steps, stopped to think in the shade under the broad porch. If Will Chalk was taken care of, it would dispose of the only witness against him ... the only eye witness. If done properly, Bluestem would be his. With the dam then taken apart, water would find its way back down Cholla Creek. Five minutes later he watched Foote and Shoeville heading towards the distant canyon, then he called to Deavis.

'Get some men together,' he said, still looking towards the two riders. 'I want the Chalk feller moved on ... or down. And the other one. Whatever his name is.'

'OK, Boss. What about *them*?' Twixt a grimace and a grin, Deavis showed his darkly stained teeth, jerked his head towards Shoeville and Foote.

'Leave them be. But send a man into town to warn Mower.'

10

At mid-afternoon Preston Mower was restless and impatient. He walked down to the corrals and looked over the horses, hoped it wouldn't be long before Ogden sent a crew to collect them.

'You're feeding these broncs too much,' he said to the wrangler. 'You're stuffin' them at my expense. Leave out the oats.' He looked around at the town, decided to walk across to the Bello Hotel. Two cowhands from Far Creek appeared to be asleep on the porch, and he rapped one of them on the foot.

'How'd you boys like to make a few dollars?' he asked. 'It's more fun inside than out here.'

In unison, two faces appeared from beneath range hats. 'Doing what?' one of them asked.

'Running broomtails to Bolas.'

'We like it out here,' the second man replied, and the hats went back to covering their faces.

'I'll make it worthwhile.'

'*This* is worthwhile. Go an' tend your store, you tight-fisted son-of-a-bitch,' the man concluded.

It was hot on the street and Mower turned irritably into the Bello Hotel. He drifted into a poker game, lost ten dollars in short order, and tramped back to Todo

Mercantile. By first dark he had worked off his nervousness on a freighter captain who had wanted credit and a young-ster who had asked for a dip in the lemon sugar can. Now, from across the street, he eyed the quiet sheriff's office and jailhouse.

Ten minutes later he leaned back in Turner Foote's chair and surveyed the office. The sheriff's gun belts hanging from a peg caught his eye. He thought back to the incident when Bluestem's ramrod had obligated Foote on to the big mare and out of town. He recalled Foote and the rifle, wondered why a Colt revolver had been left behind under lock and key.

Turner Foote was the fourth partner. But he was a man fortified by jugs of cheap liquor and the thought of immi-nent profit; a man easily swayed and easily scared. Consequently, Mower was concerned that Ben Shoeville might worry Foote into saying too much. It was scant con-solation knowing that Shoeville was on Bolas land, that Bruno Ogden wouldn't knowingly let such an opportunity slip by. But what if Ogden decided to play the cards as they were dealt?

Mower almost broke into a run in his haste to get away, almost ignoring his sales helper and the customers. He usually carried a hideaway revolver, but spared the idea when he considered Shoeville's competence with mechan-ics and the like. He took a new rifle from the rack and with an unsteady hand thumbed shells into the chamber. He returned to his office and left by the rear door, and hurried to the livery.

The rising trail was long, dusty and hot. Leading his horse, Mower walked most of it. When they came to the crest the trader paused to quarter the land. Under the hunter's moon he could see for nearly a mile. Behind him was White Mesa, while ahead and below were dry washes of the creeks.

He nestled himself among a string of flat rocks to ponder the problem of Turner Foote. It wouldn't be a ticket to Whiterod, where cheap and available liquor would loosen his tongue, and not out to Bolas where he would be more than an inconvenience. Mower decided it was best the sheriff was right out of the picture. Maybe going the same way as Elmer Broad . . . maybe from this very spot.

Placing the rifle alongside him, Mower felt his decision was crucial, and curiously justified.

Ben Shoeville didn't look back as he rode with Turner Foote through the canyon into open country. He was thinking things through – like Preston Mower, taking stock. He'd had qualms all along about bringing the law into it. His gut instinct was to shoot Ogden and take his chance on a getaway into and through Condor Pass. That was an odds-on advantage, the cold shoulder to Foote's futile law.

Nursing their own vinegary silences, the pair jogged on, the Flats around them featureless and colourless in the failing light. Shoeville looked about him like a man concerned at the order of the land, the diverted watercourse prevailing above all else. 'Hey – if word was to reach Tyler's Post, I'd wager the army would make a gallup,' he said.

'Why? Why'd they do that?' Foote replied, drawing back.

'To quell a civil uprising . . . the start of a range war. Do you think Bluestem's goin' to sit back and watch a land grab without lifting a gun? Me included?'

Foote shook his head. 'If you ask me, it's more to do with those two rollin' stones you hired. I'll turn over some ol' dodgers, see if I can find anythin'.'

'Don't get dust up your nose,' Shoeville offered derisively. He gripped the saddlehorn in anger, the knuckles of his hands gleaming in the dusk. 'If you're wanting a killer, take a good look at Bolas. Your friend Ogden's got a whole gangload of them on his payroll.'

Foote looked nonplussed towards Shoeville. 'There's not one hell of a lot I can do now,' he said, the thought almost amusing him.

'Yeah. If I didn't know better I'd think there was a satisfied smile messing with your face, Sheriff.' Shoeville leaned forward for effect. 'I'll be riding to Whiterod. That's where the Bruno Ogden Land and Stock Company's registered. Ogden is only one of the principals, or has us believe. So I want to find out who the others might be. With the help of the land agent, commissioner *and* marshal's office, if needs be, I'll get this goddamn business sorted.'

'And Mollie Broad knows about this?'

'Not yet, she doesn't. But I've had it on my mind for a while,' Shoeville said. 'Maybe Will Chalk was right in saying to give the law a try.' He heard, rather than saw, Foote's sharp turn towards him. 'That surprise you, does it? I wonder if it was *you* he meant to get included in all that, Sheriff? Then he don't know you like we all do.'

'It's more'n a hornet's nest you're pokin' at.' Foote was now more fearful. 'Why not give Ogden a chance? I reckon he's got the message if he's up to no good. Maybe he'll think better of it all by mornin',' he suggested anxiously.

'An' maybe one day we'll be calling you Mr President,' Shoeville scowled his contempt for Foote. 'Ogden's men are already looking for Chalk and Latchford, and they won't be wanting town gossip.' He swung his horse in close to Foote's mare. 'But right now it's home for me, and that's Bluestem,' he said. 'I reckon you can find your way from here . . . straight to the Bello Hotel's bar.'

The sheriff put his horse to the steep cut-bank, clopped dully across the bed of the dry wash. As the big chestnut mare climbed the opposite bank, faltering with weariness, a figure detached itself from the ground shadows. The silvery moonlight gleamed on the rifle barrel of the man who'd been waiting, and Turner Foote reached for his own weapon.

'Sheriff,' the voice called out.

Foote groaned. 'What the hell, Mower,' he gasped nervously. 'I saw the glint o' your rifle . . . could've plugged you. What the hell you doin' out here?'

'Waitin' for you.'

Foote heeled his horse forwards, tight reined as the animal tried to evade Mower. 'Must be important . . . to leave dollars behind.'

Mower wanted to retort with something about getting separated from a jug of drunk water but he ignored the mockery. He took in the sheriff's nervousness and grinned coldly. 'Where's Shoeville gone?'

'Bluestem. Then he's goin' to Whiterod . . . nearest US marshal.' Foote swung wearily to the ground, stamped some numbness from his legs. 'Goddamn him. An' I'm too long in the game for these hours in the saddle.'

Set in pasty features, Mower's eyes narrowed. He smacked the barrel of his rifle against his leg. 'Who the hell gave him that idea?' he said accusingly.

'You don't think it was me, do you?' Foote rasped. 'You think I want the administration o' the whole Territory comin' to town? What's goin' to happen when they discover who precisely owns the Bolas company . . . the responsible parties?'

Implications quickly touched the trader. 'Is that what he's after?'

'It's what he said.'

'Then he'll have to be stopped. Does Ogden know?'

'No. An' listenin' to you, it's hardly likely is it?'

'It's got to be someone we can trust.' Mower looked intently at Foote. 'Someone who knows how to disappear afterwards. It's more your line o' business, goddamnit. Who can you think of?'

'No one,' Foote barked. 'The bit about trust makes it impossible. This is Hog Valley. Besides, we can't kill off everyone from Bluestem. I want no more part of it,' he added.

'We have to stick together,' Mower charged. 'The four of us.'

'Three.' Foote gathered up the reins and climbed awkwardly into the saddle, missed the twist of anger in Mower's face. 'This ain't my work anymore. I'm pullin' out,' he said.

Mower didn't say any more, just watched Foote ride away. He waited until he saw the sheriff silhouetted against the darkening skyline, then he lifted his rifle, slowly, deliberately eased back the hammer.

'An' I'm pullin' this,' he called out, more to himself than Foote. He sighted the target, and without hesitation squeezed the trigger.

The hard, flat crack of the rifle shot split the vast silence. Then there was a visceral, dull thud as the bullet struck Foote in the middle of his back. The impact drove him forwards, lifeless, head first down from his saddle. The mare ran, broke into a frightened gallop until Mower's second shot brought her to her knees.

Mower's glance searched the ever-increasing darkness, but the dying horse's last strides had carried it just beyond any clear vision. Levering up more shells, he shot another four times, fast, covering the ground where he thought the horse had finally fallen. 'Certainty's better than hopin'. I'm a goddamn storekeeper,' he muttered.

Ben Shoeville recognized the sound of a Winchester and pulled his horse into a slow walk. He dropped further down to the dried-up bed, hugged the rocky bankside shadows that screened him from sight. He counted the shots and accepted his thoughts of the rifle, sat quietly cursing, his mind racing with curiosity.

A slight sense of missing out on something stirred him then, and he climbed back up the bank in the direction of White Mesa. He saw two formless shapes up ahead, ground-hitched his horse and walked cautiously forward. He kneeled and rolled Turner Foote on to his side, his curses returning at the sight of where the sheriff had been back-shot. Bruno Ogden was a man who could make this sort of killing – murder a lawman who had to have his mouth kept shut.

He stood up, silent, unmoving. There was a sound, a horse nickered close by. 'Whoever you are, I'm probably on your side,' he called out, lying in an attempt to gain an advantage.

In the continued silence, he decided not to push. He walked back to his mare, climbed into the saddle and loped towards the crossing. Almost immediately there was a flash of light and a shot from up ahead. The mare snorted and stumbled and he threw himself sideways. The gun fired a second time and pain hammered through him, numbing his reactions for a moment after he landed.

He drew his revolver and fired into the gloom, towards where he thought the gunshot had come from. There was an immediate return of fire that tore past his shoulder, hit a hard place behind him and ricocheted. He scrambled to his feet and lurched towards his horse, bent low and biting his lip to counter the pain. The mare skittered to one side, but he reached out and grabbed the reins, dragged himself to within reach of the saddle.

The next shot felt as though he'd been whacked hard by a shovel. It knocked the breath from his body and he fell hard against the mare. *This is how you did for Lewis Redbone as well as Foote,* were his thoughts as he slipped to the ground, still gripping his Colt.

In pain and anguish, he heard someone riding away. 'Don't go, you son-of-a-bitch,' he whispered hoarsely. 'Come an' see if I'm dead yet.'

Again, he dragged himself to his horse. But the animal was frightened, spooked, and it crow-hopped at the smell of his blood. Then the deep dark enveloped him, his thoughts and hurt fading quickly as he sank to the ground.

11

Lightning slashed the sky far beyond Condor Pass. Dark stormclouds were piling up over the San Andreas mountains. On the Bluestem side of the range the air was hot and humid, hardly any movement or sound.

Latchford Loke was waiting, sitting out of sight in a thicket of greasewood. He slapped irritatedly at the pestering flies, dabbed at beads of sweat across his forehead. He heard nothing, yet knew that the danger was growing. Twice in the past hour a flurry of rising quail let him know that men were somewhere out there. Like him they were waiting, so he continued to sit in edgy silence.

He waited another thirty minutes. Suddenly he leaned with his ear close to the ground, heard the measured tread of a carefully ridden horse.

Clamping on his battered range hat, Latch scurried to his waiting mount. In the saddle, he awkwardly hauled his carbine from under his left leg, and placed it across his lap. He sat and watched the dark shape become more visible, and his nervousness eased.

'Yeah, they're there all right, Latch.' Will Chalk's voice was cool and unhurried. 'More'n you could shake a stick at.' The man squinted at his partner, his mouth forming a near cheerful grin.

With excitement now replacing the dull ache of his shoulder wound, Latch was stirred. 'Hells clangin' bangin' bells, Will. What are we waitin' for?'

'To stop the both of us getting shot dead, that's what.' Will was calculating, as he thought back. 'There's a pair on point, maybe three. One or two to drive the beef out. That means anything we figure on doing, must be done before Bolas has a chance to gather up.'

'So let's go get 'em. It's our beef . . . sort of.'

'You've been sitting in the sun too long,' Will said as he slid from the saddle. He hunkered down, stared off across the flats. 'There's near a thousand head. That's a peck o' trouble . . . more if you consider the opposition.'

Under a dash of lightning, the shape of the country momentarily came clear and sharp. Will saw the canyon that marked the hideout of the beef. It had been late afternoon when they had seen Shoeville and Foote heading that way. By now, Shoeville should have been on the way out. But Bruno Ogden was no fool, and if he told the sheriff to haul ass, the lawman would have done. Ben Shoeville would be left alone and Foote wouldn't lift a finger of help, let alone show a badge.

'Hell, I'd kick my own dog if I had one,' Latch mumbled in frustration as he walked towards Will. He stood for a few moments glowering, issuing threats and imprecations. Then he lowered his chin, stared thoughtfully at the shapes of greasewood that close dotted the range. He took a step aside, bent down, snapped off a twig and a leaf, smelled at the oily sap and grinned. 'You reckon there's a way into the Bolas graze from here?' he asked.

'Yes and no. It's wired,' Will said. 'Three strands of good

ol' bobwire . . . shoulder high.'

'Then they've got to cut it to let the beef through.' Latch reached out, his gnarled fingers flicked across Will's arm. 'If it's trouble we're stayin' for in this godforsaken place, we've hit gold, Will. I'm tired an' dry, an' I ain't got the humour to stand here wastin' more wind, so let's make our play.' Latch put the greasewood twig between his teeth. 'You can suck on this for your afflictions,' he explained. 'Ain't no wives' tale, neither.'

Suddenly, as if from a long vent in the earth itself, a thick dust cloud rolled out from the canyon. Lowing and bawling filled the air, and a thousand head of beef ran into the wide dry reaches of Bluestem.

'Speak o' the Devil.' Latch pointed, stared across the valley as the lightning flashed and shattered again. 'Did you see it?' he rasped. 'Looks like Hell's decided to move itself.'

Will was back on his feet, climbing into the saddle. He pulled his carbine from the scabbard, levered up a shell and lifted the reins. 'Their guards'll hear nothing above this clamour. Let's cut the valley.'

Side by side they raced down the rim, cutting across the empty flats, their horses impulsively swerving at the last moment to avoid rocks and stands of cholla. To the south, the Condor Pass was close, and Will estimated if they could make the rising peaks, they would be safe. But temporarily.

Under the silvery mantle of moonlight, Latch glanced at his partner's stern face, decided on a risky move in the hope of diverting a Bolas attack.

'We'll split up,' he said, breathlessly, dragging his horse to a stop. 'I'll watch out on this side. You do the same from the other side o' the herd.'

Will shook his head slowly. 'We'll do it together,' he decided.

Latch reciprocated with the head shake. 'One man can move in and out better'n two. You know that, Will. When the beef shows, we'll stir 'em up.'

'It ain't right,' Will continued.

Latch smiled. 'There's nothin' much about all this that is. An' we don't want to add wastin' time,' he countered kindly.

The deep earthy rumble was getting closer. Latch's horse had its head up, its ears pricked, snorting anxiously. Another colossal ribbon of lightning from south to east made the whole thing stark and clear. A low weaving cloud of noise, steers with lowered heads and raking horns tearing through the sea of cholla and greasewood.

'OK,' Will conceded. 'But if anything happens to you tonight . . . anything more than it has already, I'll ride into Bolas and gun down Ogden myself . . . no questions.'

'That's touchin', Will. It figures on my wish list.'

Latch waited until Will had crossed the mouth of the canyon before taking up his position. Then, with an earnest grin across his face he calmly began to snap branches of greasewood. The wood was brittle and dry and it only took minutes to create a balled heap of boughs. He lashed up the greasewood bundle, paid out his reata and fastened it to the cantle of his saddle. Then he stood for more waiting.

Under the ghostly blanket of moonlight, Latch saw the canyon floor filled with patchy goosefoot, broken thickets of mesquite. He nodded favourably. The herd was approaching, the ground was in a deeper tremble and the pall of dust was rising.

The Bluestem stock was pouring down the north side of the arroyo. The heavily armed Bolas riders were slapping quirts, waving lariats as they urged the beef into wild flight towards the canyon.

Latch waited until he was certain there could be no turning back or veering off course. He mounted his horse and struck a vesta, held it until the flame caught at the greasewood, with a shout of success moved forward. The blazing mesh of wood was dragged through the dry brush, flames rearing and spreading behind him. It was a wall of fire for turning the herd back on to Bluestem soil, not Bruno Ogden's Bolas.

Confused yells penetrated the darkness. Riders waving catch ropes grouped on the north side of the herd, two of them with wire-cutters dashed towards the fence.

Will Chalk's rifle crashed out from the rimrock and one man fell, another went down as his horse stumbled and fell beneath him. The cattle were now spilling down into the canyon, pushed on by the relentless, troubled herd behind them. The belt of flames was leaping higher, rolling towards the inevitable.

The Bolas men had their blood up. Oaths and what sounded like battlecries cut through the thundering hoofs, bullets zipped and whined everywhere. Backlit by the low flames, Latch raced on across the canyon mouth, igniting the dry weeds and brush. Sparrows and bushtits were scattered from their nightly roosts, desert critters scuttled for alternative cover and safety.

Left alone after being herded into the canyon, the herd would have gone straight on, disappeared, scattered into Condor Pass. Now, unable to face the wall of glaring heat and flames, the cattle were running to the north. Bawling and bellowing, the herd leaders pressed and harried the mob away, scorched, frightened animals anxious for any shelter in the night.

Latch rode on, swerving his horse through the darkness until he was high on the opposite slope. He flipped the end of the reata from his saddlehorn, yelled a greeting as Will arrived silhouetted against the reddening glow.

Latch took off his hat, swiped at the ash powder around his shoulders and legs. 'I've been breathin' this goddamn stuff,' he remarked. 'Let's get the hell out o' here. I feel like a lump o' jerky.'

Hours had passed since the horses had watered. Latch lifted his waterbag off the saddle, poured water into his hat and wet the mare's lips and mouth. 'Sorry, we ain't finished yet,' he growled. He swabbed the horse's nostrils, waited until it sucked the hat dry. 'There's a few more miles to go.'

'Where'd you reckon you'll be going then, Latch? Do you hear that?' Will nodded out to the valley where a handful of riders were at a headlong gallop in the direction of the Bluestem ranch. 'They're not out for any promenade,' he said, drily.

The two men waited silently as the others rode on, squinting against the darkness as the noise of the Bolas riders faded across the swags and hog wallows.

'No, it's us they're after,' Latch agreed. 'But their mounts won't make it much further. Their hearts'll bust afore they catch anythin'.'

'We could be on our knees ourselves before morning's out,' Will said.

'I'm hopin' for a cold beer in town.' Latch spat something from the corner of his mouth. 'The Big Bella, wasn't it?' he asked and spat again noisily.

'Near enough,' Will replied. 'Tell me about Henri.'

'He's in the barn with a rifle for a nurse.' Latch dropped his reins, rubbed the palm of his hand around his wrinkled face. 'There's half o' that ol' Frenchman just itchin' for a Bolas scalp.'

'We didn't see Ben Shoeville ride away from Bolas.' Will

reminded Latch. 'Do you reckon Ogden will cut him down?'

'Not with a town sheriff as witness.' Latch heeled his horse into a canter. 'The way I see it, the only chance we've got is go to town, then come back again along the White Mesa road.'

'After you've had that dust cutter,' Will prodded.

'Yep. I gave my horse the last water.' Latch paused. 'Besides, I'm out o' that chaw baccy.'

'You've never used it.'

'From now on I'm goin' to. Reckon I've been driven to it.'

When they reached the edge of town, they rode to the bridge, drew into the deep shadow of a cotton-wood as two horsemen crossed the creek. They continued, took a side street until they levelled with Preston Mower's mercantile, rode on to the Bello Hotel.

Four horses were hitched outside the hotel saloon, and as Will and Latch dismounted and tied in their own mounts, the smack of horse sweat and scorched hair was unmistakable. Bolas riders had made town before them.

Latch stood and listened for a few moments. He caught Will's quizzical glance, who shrugged. 'Go on then,' he said, 'We haven't rode here for nothing.'

They blinked as they stepped into the bright lamplight of the bar. Latch moved to the left, Will to the right of the door. Two Bolas riders stood close to the bar, one nearer the door, one in the far corner, among the poker tables. The barkeep shuddered, cursed under his breath as Latch moved towards him. He glanced at his under-the-counter shotgun, the cellar door to shield him from firearms trouble.

'Two beers,' Latch snapped a coin on the bar, grinned at his seedy, battered reflection in the back-bar mirror.

'We've worked up a wet appetite.'

Will had already noted, recognized one or two of the Bolas men. He was hoping maybe they were thinking as he was. That they weren't too aware of the recent confrontation in the canyon.

Copper John pushed his empty glass away, removed an elbow from the soggy bar top. His right hand hung at his side, the tips of his fingers fidgeting close to a Colt's revolver. His nose twitched and he winked at Mal Deavis. 'You always know when there's a Bluestem waddy around. Only time they see a bath's if they fall in the goddamn dippin' chute,' he said abusively.

Latch swallowed, stared at Copper John over the rim of the glass. 'Ain't that the truth,' he replied disarmingly, placing his beer down carefully in front of him. He shifted his glance from one man to the other, a slow, chilly smile stirring beneath his whiskery moustache. 'You heifer brands fresh from a town social?' he asked.

'If you Bluestems are takin' on trouble. . . .' Copper John started, taking a further step away from the bar. 'I'll oblige you,' the man added, his wariness including Will.

'You ain't paid for breakages.' the barkeep's anxious shout cut through the miasma of smoke, booze fumes and sweat. 'Fight outside.'

'We'll do it here,' Latch rasped. 'Losers pay for the damage. Ain't no mouthy cow chaser separatin' me from my beer.'

In the sudden charged silence, they all heard the horse pounding up the quiet street, the breaking of the hitch rail, the thud of something falling. Will backed up to the swing doors, elbowed one of them open. In the darkness, he saw Ben Shoeville's mount lying on its side, the saddle and mane bloody and shiny in the pool of yellow lamplight. There was no sign of a rider.

Will drew his Colt and stepped out on to the veranda, a small crowd following to the street behind him.

'There he is,' a man gasped. 'He's down . . . hurt.'

It was Ben Shoeville, crawling from the street, hatless and covered with a crust of blood. As he reached out for the boardwalk he grunted and fell forward, twisted, sitting in the hard-packed dirt with his shoulders against the raised timbers.

Will was the first to reach him. 'Who did this?' he asked, holstering his gun, kneeling close.

'I don't know.' The words were slow and painful as Shoeville stared up at Will. 'Never do. It's the way of 'em. They got Foote. Used a rifle . . . a Winchester.'

The small crowd moved aside as Preston Mower pushed through. 'What's he said?' The big trader's face was twisted with anger. 'Yesterday, it was him who swore to gun the sheriff.'

'Well, today it looks like it's someone else,' Latch snarled back from the boardwalk.

Copper John and Deavis were now looking on, sullenly. They stood either side of Mower, close, as if some deed or thought was passing between them.

'I reckon Mr Mower here's suddenly got himself another job . . . the sheriff's duties.' Deavis grinned. 'He's not the best liked, but there's no law I know of says you have to be that. He's certainly well known enough among the White Mesa community.' He gave the trader a deadpan look. 'You've just been elected. Start your duty.'

Mower's eyes narrowed. 'I'll deputize you two until we can have an election. So get Shoeville to the jailhouse. An' tell the doc.'

'You'll take him to the surgery, you scum.' Will's right hand moved to his Colt, but he held steady when the two doubtful incumbents thumbed back the hammers of their own handguns.

'There'll be a trial. If you've somethin' to say, say it then.' Mower strode off towards the jail, left his two deputies to organize disquiet on the street.

12

Threatened by Mal Deavis's gun, the glimmer of success for Bolas, Will stood quite still, carefully looked over the hushed knot of citizens. Whatever opinion they held, they were expediently reserving any show of support.

'Shoeville's not a killer. Most of you should know that,' he stated forcefully.

Copper John glanced from Will to Latch. He walked around Deavis and stood looking down at Shoeville's horse. Drawing the rifle from the saddle scabbard he levered the action, picked up the empty shell case that fell at his feet. 'Well, this has been fired,' he said.

'Hell, what do you expect of a man when someone takes a cowardly shot at his back? Turn over to have his belly tickled?' There was real scorn in Will's reply.

Deavis shot back his own response. 'We'll take care o' that. You just heard, there's a bunch of us aim to do Foote's job for him.'

'I heard there's two of you,' Will corrected. 'Do it legal, for Chris'sakes.' Will looked around the group of men. 'An' make sure Shoeville gets that doc. If he dies, he won't be alone.'

Will untied his snorty mount from the broken hitch rail

and walked it down the street.

'You goin' to leave him there?' Latch wanted to know. 'What's come over you, Will?'

'Nothing. Ben's hurt bad, but what more can we do? They'll get him to a doc. Miss Broad can tend to him after that. She's conveniently placed, don't forget.'

His features setting hard, Will walked on, back past the mercantile. Almost kicking the dirt in frustration, his entire being was fighting a desire to turn around and cut loose on the Bolas crew.

Alerted by the commotion in the main street, Mollie Broad was standing at the picket gate of Marge Highgate's house. She saw them coming and ran forward.

'Where's Ben?' she called out. 'Has something happened? Has Ogden got to him?'

'Yeah, he had a damn good try. Him and Foote got themselves bushwhacked,' Will answered, reaching out to grip Mollie by the wrist. 'Mower's getting Ben to the doc's. He's wounded bad and needs some surgery. After that, you can see he's taken care of.'

Mollie looked up. With tears in her eyes she nodded. 'Yes, of course . . . all I can.' She blinked hard, her jaw set with rising bitterness. 'You said Mower. What's it got to do with him?'

'He's the new sheriff. Acting sheriff. Most out there seemed to agree he was the man for the job. He's not my choice.'

'Nor mine,' Mollie agreed. 'Not even in desperation.'

The house door banged to, and Marge Highgate advanced on the group. 'What's going on out here? Who's this?' she asked.

When Mollie had explained, made introductions, Will continued quietly. 'I'm sure you're safe enough here, and Ogden's not going to try anything with witnesses. We would have brought Ben with us, but he's too hurt for that. Besides, we've got some riding to do.'

Mollie considered the predicament for a moment. She looked at Marge then back to Will. 'What about Henri?'

'We're going back for him now,' he said, watching with curiosity as Marge hurried off, away from the house.

'Yeah. Well, we cut your beef loose. Now they're spread half way across Hog Flats. Ogden's going to play hell rounding 'em up. He might even have to hire some punchers, instead of gunslingers.'

Will pulled his horse forwards, hesitated. 'Like I said . . . Latch and me's got things to do before morning comes.'

'Call it off, Will.' Mollie's voice was suddenly lower, more apprehensive. 'Just stop now. God knows, I never counted on a range war, or anything like it.'

'Pah,' Latch rasped. 'Don't bring Him into it. Ogden started this, an' we'll finish it. I say we get goin'.'

'After Bluestem,' Will spoke hurriedly. 'Ogden sent those canyon guards to patrol the Cholla. They'll kill Henri if they find him.'

'There's a line cabin . . . corner of Bluestem and Far Creek. You'll find it easy enough. Take him there. I'll keep in touch somehow.'

Minutes later, Marge reappeared out of the darkness. She stood listening to Mollie's directions, looked disdainfully at Will and Latch. 'You figure to shove against Bolas? Reckon you'll need more than what you got so far, fellers,' she said. 'And you'll get this girl killed.'

Will climbed into his saddle, held his horse on a tight rein 'No, we won't,' he replied briskly. 'I want the man who shot Foote. And I want him before the new sheriff considers taking Ben to Whiterod. Ma'am,' he added with a tip of his hat.

*

Henri stared around the hayloft, caught a glimpse of starlight through the boards of the warped roof. For a while he tried to bring back what had happened to him, but he couldn't recall much more than Bruno Ogden's distant voice and a hammer blow to the back of his head. He twisted on his side and the pain made him gasp. Then he smelled sour mescal, felt the dressed wound around his neck.

A gnashing, munching sound from below filled the barn and he held his breath for a moment. He recognized the noise of a feeding horse, crawled to the edge of the loft and stared down at his rimrock mare. But then an outbreak of guttural laughter came from the house and he struggled back to the side wall, raised himself to peer through the window. The house veranda was lit by wall sconces, and in the outer reach of the glow he could see four saddled horses. The ranch-house door slammed and a man came out on to the veranda, leaned on a rail and listened.

Henri muttered a curse and felt around in the hay. Lifting his shotgun, he broke it open, saw the glint of two 12-gauge cartridges. Then he slumped down with his head against the wall and waited.

A slight breeze drifted through the barn, bringing with it the aroma of frying meat. Despite the distress of his suffering, Henri was weak with hunger, and he longed painfully for a drink. The men inside the house were talking loudly, but he heard a horse come into the yard. He peered around the frame of the window, his fingers flexing tight around the shotgun when Ogden's face showed yellow in the lamplight.

'Deavis come back yet?' the man called out from the foot of the steps.

The ranchhouse door opened and a Bolas rider stepped

out. 'He went into town with Copper John, boss.'

'So get those horses under cover.' Ogden's manner was abrupt. 'Run them into the barn.'

Henri got to his feet, his back pressed against the wall as he fought down the waves of sickness. He heard the sound of boots on gravel outside the barn door. Then the horses came in and the dry dust wafted up into the roof space.

'Boose – Joe Boose.' Ogden's voice came from close by, outside now. 'Keep an eye open for Chalk. And there's probably two of them. They'll show up here, unless Deavis gets in first.'

'Hell, I was just goin' to eat,' the man named Boose protested. 'There's food inside. I can smell it.'

'If there is, I'll get some sent out. Remember what I said.'

When Ogden had gone, Boose came into the barn. He scratched a vesta and the flare was blindingly bright after the darkness.

Henri gently laid the shotgun aside. He flexed the muscles of his right hand, but made no move towards the big old pistol that hung at his side. He licked his parched lips, the light went out, and again Henri waited patiently; he didn't have to wait long before another Bolas man walked into the barn.

'Is that my chuck? What is it?' Boose asked disagreeably.

'Hump rib, with sweet onions an' taters. Then there's apple pie an' cream with a glass o' cold branch water. What the hell do you think it is?' the man gruffed. 'It's fried beef an' beans.'

'Do you know how long I'm supposed to stay here?' Boose continued.

'An hour maybe. Someone will let you know,' the man answered, and hurried back to the house.

In his right hand, Henri gripped his .44 Army Colt. An

hour, the man had said, and first light wasn't far off. He slid the weapon into his holster and buttoned down the flap. He crawled back across the puncheon flooring, stopped and cursed silently at realizing dusty shards of hay were falling through the wide gaps in the boards.

Boose paused in his eating, stood up with his hand on the butt of his Colt. A horse sneezed and kicked out a front leg. The Bolas gunman grunted and sat down again.

But Henri was ready, positioned for the moment he needed. He stepped off the holding beam and went straight down, his feet spread to make contact with either side of Boose's neck. He felt his fall ending with the snap of collar bones, then a stab of pain rising from his own feet, up his body to his head. Joe Boose had made no sound. He lay crumpled with his plate of food, his upper body cracked and broken.

Henri's legs buckled and he toppled forwards, down on his knees then on all fours. He crawled away from the man's body and staggered to his feet. In the cloying darkness he was stunned and disorientated, drew in long breaths, again gasping at the hurt. He moved towards the horses, feeling his way in the dark. His hands reached out for a saddle, the sheath of a carbine, to one side for the reins.

He led the horse in a half-circle, straight out of the barn. Beyond the range of the home yard he pulled himself up into the saddle, gritted his teeth against a rising wave of sickness.

'You might as well run. I'm not going to notice,' he muttered to the horse, and cursed a metis epithet as the animal responded down into and along the dried-up Cholla Creek. He let his head fall forwards, was quietly sick on to the horse's damp neck. Suddenly everything gave way and he felt himself toppling sideways. As he fell, he carried a fleeting thought about mountain cats writhing and twisting in mid-air to land on their feet. He didn't have time to grin, only to see the dark hazy shapes of two riders close by, watching him. He tried to say something, to ask what was going on, but nothing came.

'Looks like he's been in more wars . . . got nothin' left.' Latchford Loke's's voice cut through the foggy mist and Henri smiled weakly.

'Ease along there,' a harder voice warned. 'You're staying right where you are for the moment.'

'There's four . . . five, back at Bluestem,' Henri mumbled in return.

'Yeah, we guessed as much.' Will and Latch pushed the half-conscious man back into the saddle, held him until Latch hitched his wrists to the saddlehorn. Then the three of them rode steadily into the hills, towards the soft pink light that stretched between the distant San Andreas Mountains and Condor Pass.

13

Leaving Bluestem, Bruno Ogden rode into town to seek out Mal Deavis. He was having trouble accepting the way Will Chalk and Latchford Loke had, to all intents and purposes, stolen the herd. They had stampeded the beef under the gun barrels of six Bolas men on fighting wages. He had a grudging admiration for Will Chalk. *A couple like him on my payroll, and I wouldn't be a goddamn rustler to get where I'm going . . . that's for sure,* ran through his mind. But that thought was tempered by the fact that Mollie Broad had outsmarted him.

While he was in White Mesa he would look for Turner Foote as well as Deavis. Foote had been sheriff for three years, two of which he had been in the pay of the Bruno Ogden Land and Stock Company. So Ogden kept thinking of what he would be saying. He wanted to know why the sheriff had apparently turned – into cowardice, because the lawman had to be talked out of quitting.

He entered the town from the main trail, leaving his sorrel at the jail's hitch-rack. He opened the office door and stood a moment, letting his eyes adjust to the dimness. Foote wasn't there, but in his chair sat Preston Mower.

'Good morning.' Ogden tossed his hat onto a chair beside the sheriff's desk. 'Obviously the sheriff's not around,' he said.

'No. He's in a back room of the Bello.' There was a strange look to the trader's flabby features. 'We'll plant him later today,' he added coldly.

Ogden lifted his hat from the chair and sat down. 'What the hell happened?' he asked in bafflement.

'Not entirely sure. He was comin' from your place, last night.' Mower's voice held an undercurrent of fear, just discernible in his expression. 'They must have had an argument. Shoeville gunned him.'

Ogden was silent, thoughtful for a long moment. 'What else?' he asked.

'Well, Foote *was* sheriff . . . usually gave him the edge. He got bullets into Shoeville . . . managed to finish off his horse, too. We got him here . . . in the jailhouse.'

'How about Deavis and Copper John? Are they around here?'

'Over at the saloon, last I saw. They're standin' ready in case Shoeville tries to break out.'

The storekeeper looked hard at Ogden. 'An' afore you ask, I got the job of lawman until somethin' turns up.'

'It doesn't sound as if Shoeville's going far with two of Foote's bullets in him.' Ogden sneered derisively and got to his feet, leaned intimidatingly close to Mower. 'There's about as much lard there as there is on your store prices, Mower. You're lying through your teeth.'

Mower rose defensively fast. 'It was a killin', an' like I told you. It was those trigger men o' yours who found him.'

'But who told them where to look, Mower?'

Mower started back, his eyes slitted and treacherous. 'Half the goddamn town witnessed what happened here.'

'Yeah, I'm sure they did, you son-of-a-bitch,' Ogden growled. 'But who witnessed the killing? Let *me* tell you like it is,' the Bolas man continued. 'Foote and Shoeville rode into Bolas together. Shoeville was spitting tacks, but he'd settle for the go-ahead to look at the Bolas herds. He was after Bluestem strays . . . even offered a few men for the tally. He wasn't interested in gunplay . . . not at that point.'

Ogden pushed Mower back down into his chair. 'It was about then that the good sheriff's more spineless side started to show. I know he was nervous of those two fellers Mollie Broad had hired. He said he was finished with his job, and he meant it. I thought he'd be coming back to town to get roostered.'

'You're tryin' to intimidate me into somethin', Bruno. I know it. But you're not goin' to.' Mower attempted to assert himself. 'I'd a quarter interest that's now a third. Turner Foote might have been content to walk out . . . go back for some small bunce to top up his lawman's pension. But not me. I'm not goin' anywhere.'

Ogden raised the chilliest of smiles. 'How'd you know he was walking out? I didn't say that. Was it fear made you shoot him? Another Elmer Broad number, eh? More bullets in the back. How long was it before Shoeville came back and you had to shoot him too?'

'The man was goin' to sell you out . . . sell us all out.' Mower was stiff with worry. He put a shaking hand to his face, wiped across his mouth. 'For Chris'sakes, Bruno, I tried to talk him out of it, but he went for his gun.'

'That's what they all say. Had no choice.'

'Keep your voice down,' Mower said, looking towards the cells. 'I told you, Shoeville's in there. The doc's been tendin' him. So, Foote's dead,' he continued. 'Well, he might have got shot by anybody. He wouldn't have been without enemies. It might've been on account o' nothin' more'n Shoeville's anger. He got prised away from here . . . him an' his friend the titty bottle. There would've been a witness or two saw that.'

'That man Chalk's no fool,' Ogden said. 'Him and the other one rode into Bluestem last night and took that old metis up into the hills somewhere. The place was crawling with my men, and he was on top of them . . . hiding in the goddamn hayloft.'

Mower's worry increased with the purposeful look in Ogden's eyes. 'I'll put Shoeville on the Whiterod stage when it pulls through,' he said. 'Let the law there handle things.'

'And bring investigators to Hog Flats? United States marshals looking up past killings and referencing tally books? I don't think so, you half-wit. Hell, they'll be checking the back trails of every man on my payroll! I ought to shoot you now.'

Mower sucked air through his teeth. 'If anythin' happens to me, the law will have enough evidence to hang you out to dry, Bruno. There's papers an' tally books, an' every steer what's passed through my pens has been checked an' cross checked. A balanced book. Double entry, they call it at the rail-head. Somethin' you wouldn't know about.'

Ogden eased his nickel-plated Colt from its shoulder holster. 'Maybe. But I've another way of balancing my book, Mower. Simple, single entry stuff. Besides, I can always burn Todo Mercantile down. That should rid us of your precious paper reckonings.'

'You're not scarin' me away from what I've gathered.'

'Then there's the girl,' Ogden continued blatantly. 'Maybe you'll have to kill her too? Like father, like daughter, eh?'

Mower considered a moment. 'I can't understand why you're so goddamn fussed about that,' he countered. 'You've been forced to make a cull before.'

'That's true enough. But no more than a handful. And

no women. That's best left to the likes of you.'

'You reckon you can collect my share of Bolas an' then ride across to the Broad place an' get that too?' Mower demanded. 'You really think that?'

'Bolas? Huh,' Ogden laughed. 'I've already got Far Creek and I'm not expecting much trouble from Bluestem. But I can pull out now if you want. Leave you and Marge to run Bolas together. That would suit, wouldn't it?'

Mower got to his feet again as a sudden thought struck him. 'Marge came in last night. Told me Chalk and company are shacked up somewhere near the snowline.'

'One of the old line cabins, probably. I'll tend to that,' Ogden said – as the street door opened and Mollie Broad entered with a gust of fierce heat off the street.

'Can I see him?' she asked without preamble.

'He's a killer,' Mower replied. 'I don't know that I should let you anywhere near.'

'He's about as much a killer as you are straight and fair-minded, Mr Mower. Let me in there.'

Ogden's mouth twisted with suppressed mirth. 'Nothing much wrong with your judgement lady, I'll say that.' With that, he donned his hat and walked from the office, slamming the door behind him.

'I'll have to search you,' Mower said, with another wipe of his lips.

'If you do, I'll be one of the last things you ever touch.'

In reply, Mower said nothing, backing off towards the desk to open a drawer. 'But you'll have to be locked in,' he said, dangling keys in his hand.

'Then get on with it.' Mollie's voice was cold, devoid of any association.

When the cell door clanged behind her, Mollie stood looking down at Shoeville. She waited until the passageway door closed against Mower, then hurried across the cell, bent to the injured man. 'Ben, what are we going to do? What can I do?'

Shoeville rubbed his chin, tried to make himself easier on the crude cot. 'There's a good man in Will Chalk. Get *him* to do something.'

'OK. They're saying that Mower's going to get you aboard the Whiterod stage.'

'Well, that's a tad better than lying here waiting for Ogden's lynch mob,' Shoeville said regretfully.

'I've brought something for you.' Mollie went into a deep side pocket of her calico skirt, drew out the bone-handled pistol. 'Now you can hide it. If Ogden does come for you, you can shoot him first.'

'Mollie.' Shoeville swallowed hard. 'I didn't kill Foote. It happened just like I said, an' I'm not going to break out of here an' give Mower, or one of his deputies, the chance to shoot me down me for something I didn't do.' He was quiet for a moment. 'Where did they find the sheriff? I'll wager it was the same place they found your pa,' he said.

'How'd you mean, Ben?' Mollie's face reflected a blend of anger and uncertainty, something else. 'What are you thinking?' she asked quietly.

'Your pa was killed before Bruno Ogden showed up in Hog Valley . . . White Mesa.'

'I understand that.'

'So it's someone else we should be worried about . . . always should've been. Someone with a gutful of bitterness who's prepared to take an' destroy until the Broad name's nothing more'n a memory.' The muscles on Shoeville's jaw corded with the effort to control his emotion. 'I've had time to do some thinking, Mollie, an' no one would take to what I came up with.'

'Then this might help. Take it,' Mollie said, pushing the pistol into his hands.

'When's the stage coming?'

'Three days.' Mollie's eyes were getting brighter with anticipation. 'It's coming up from Tyler's Post.'

'Get word to Will an' tell him all this. Like I said, I've done some thinking . . . getting an idea together,' Shoeville offered. 'Tell him I'll be looking out for him somewhere on the road.'

'Are you sure? Are you up to all this, Ben?'

'Huh. "What doesn't kill you makes you stronger", your pa used to tell us. It was usually end o' the day, as we fell from our saddles, battered an' bruised, starving an' parched, too weak to stand.'

Mollie shaped a wistful smile. 'Will said I had to tell you, they cut the herd from the canyon. Do you think there's going to be a day soon that holds something good?'

'Yeah. I reckon most stuff averages out.'

Watching from a street-fronting window of the Bello Hotel, Ogden saw Mollie hurry from the jailhouse across to the livery stable. Ten minutes later, shielding her eyes against the bright sun, she emerged, turned left in the direction of Marge Highgate's house.

Sensing a confrontation was near, the man continued to wait, and when Mollie eventually reappeared in riding gear and wearing a range hat, he knew for sure.

'Deavis.' His voice was harsh as he turned back into the room. 'Gather the men. We've got some closure to make. Now.'

When he stepped out on to the boardwalk, beneath the hotel's overhang, Mollie Broad was long gone. But she was there in the distance, a small, rising curl of dust. The destination was beyond doubt, and Ogden smiled icily.

The Bolas riders were cantering past Todo Mercantile when the front door opened and Marge Highgate stepped out, hands on hips, confrontationally.

Ogden curled his lip, realized she'd been doing the same as him, watching the goings on.

'Come on over here,' she called out.

Ogden hauled in for a moment. 'Sounds like you've got yourself a dog to command,' he said, making no attempt to hide his irritation. 'Try that manner with Mower all you please, but never on me.' He kicked his sorrel cruelly, swung away in a cloud of choking dust and set off again.

14

Mollie put her horse down to the flats and kicked hard towards Bluestem. With Ben Shoeville in jail, she felt more alone than she had done for many years. The religious faction she'd grown up with, recommended a lifelong promise to one man. She knew now, that was likely going to be Ben.

Two figures emerged, ghostly and shimmering in the mirage on the colourless flats. Mollie's expectations were raised that it was Will Chalk and Latchford Loke. But her hopes were dashed when one of them lifted his hand, a gunshot cracked out and almost immediately, two more riders appeared. They were Bolas gunmen in pursuit of their quarry. If I can see them, they can see me, she thought, realizing if Ogden's bunch was out searching, then Will was probably still free.

Will had been right after all, her thoughts continued. The real trouble starts now. An Ogden-led Bolas had given ample warning of their intentions. With Ben Shoeville behind bars, Bluestem was reduced to a couple of strangers who had nothing to gain but their lives. And only if they fled Hog Flats.

Mollie pushed on. The Bolas riders were converging on her now and she knew that only down in the safety of the barracks, or up in the foothills, could she elude them. Her horse swerved in and out of a steep-walled gully and she lay prone along its neck, encouraging it in the direction of Condor Pass. She came to rolling sand hills, then a rising, angled bench which gave a clearer view of the valley. In the distance, where creeping sand met the flat, parched rangeland, she picked out the blurred smudges of her own Bluestem buildings. And Ogden's riders were there, spread in a long picket of vigilance.

Acting on impulse, Mollie took to the old cattle trail that led a tortuous route over the flats. It was the way herds were brought when the Meckler Apache had once controlled all the valley.

She saw tracks and reined in to take a closer look, speculated on whether the two horses could be those of Will and Latch. She went on, trotting her mount up a low rise for a better viewpoint, hauled back in near panic at confronting a group of dismounted Bolas riders.

She turned about, but Bruno Ogden and Copper John were already there to cut off her retreat. They sat their blowing mounts and stared her down.

'Out looking for someone, Miss Broad?' Ogden's voice was level, unruffled.

'She'll know where they're holed up,' Copper John grated.

Mollie dismounted. With the reins looped around her wrist, she walked towards Ogden, thankful that Will was still free. Copper John attempted to intercept her, but she stepped around him, loathing showing across her face.

'Tell your gunman to get out of the way, Ogden,' she said. 'I'm getting to the grinder man, not his monkey.'

Copper John looked quizzically at his boss, then turned aside. The other unhands backed off, leaving Mollie facing up to Ogden. He stopped patting his sorrel's glossy neck and pushed his Stetson back from his face.

'So much for the quality of your hirelings,' Mollie started. 'More guns than guile, eh?'

'We'll find them. There's time,' Ogden murmured. 'Shoeville's in jail for murder, and Bluestem's depleted of a workforce. I don't see there's much you can do.'

'Nor you, Ogden. Not as long as I have a single man somewhere out there,' Mollie retorted.

'They're probably half way home by now . . . wherever that is,' Ogden said and laughed.

'I wonder if you'll find it as amusing when they're suddenly standing in front of you . . . perhaps with a US marshal along. You could be in their sights right now.' Mollie looked disgustedly at the group of Bolas men. 'Was it one of these heroes who shot Sheriff Foote in the back?'

Ogden chose to let the question go as he dismounted. 'I said, we'll find them. In this country they'll probably lose themselves,' he said.

Mollie lifted her chin, peered thoughtfully out across the flats, at Condor Pass, the distant high mountains. 'In the middle of all this, Ogden, you'll grow old never getting out of harm's way.'

'Hell lady, it never would have come to this if you hadn't imported a brace of gunmen.' A sudden anger engulfed Ogden and he grasped Mollie's arm. 'Why?'

'Why? Why?' Mollie was incredulous. 'It's you who's paying these men to plunder and kill,' she countered, pulling herself free. 'But if it is like you say, then it's gunmen against gunmen.'

'The law of the open range.' Ogden tapped his shoulder-holstered Colt.

'That's more or less what Will Chalk told me, and I wouldn't listen . . . at first.'

'Ah, and now you know. And when they turn up, they'll know what to expect.'

'None of them's going to greet you with an outstretched arm . . . a handshake, Ogden.'

The Bolas men stared uncomfortably at each other. Mollie's words had touched a nerve with most of them. They knew that as long as one Bluestem rider stayed alive, their own lives would relentlessly be in peril.

'You'll be asking me to buy Bluestem before much longer,' he sneered.

'Never. I'll make it a gift charter to the Indian Affairs Bureau before selling to you.'

'Hah, what'll you gift them?' Ogden taunted. 'A two-by-four ranch house and a couple of ramshackle barns? Hell, where's the beef? The Indians with nothing have got more'n you.'

'The steers can be driven back to where they belong,' Mollie retorted. 'Perhaps there's one or two of your men would be glad to work for a straight brand.'

'Yeah, she knows where they're hidin'' all right,' Copper John snarled. 'Get her to say it, instead of all this jawbone.'

'You keep quiet.' Ogden spoke without turning his head. He was watching Mollie, saw the tough, resolute streak in her that matched his own. But it didn't make any difference. Bluestem had to be taken over, incorporated, subsumed in Bolas holdings. He'd gone too far to rein in now.

'Well, do you Miss Broad?' he asked. 'Do you know where they are?'

'No. Any case, would I likely tell you?' Mollie stood resolute, held her head erect. Surrounded by Bolas gunners, she knew the situation was bad, but she had no thought of giving in.

'No to what? You won't tell me where they are, or, you don't know where they are? Which is it?'

'No, to everything.'

'Then return to White Mesa,' he snapped and shoved her towards her horse. 'Show up anywhere near here again, and I'll let my men deal with the problem.'

'This is my land,' Mollie flared. 'You put the boundary of Bolas at the Cholla . . . and that's a way off my place. If you trespass here again, I'll avoid any sheriff or marshal's office and report to the army at Tyler's Post. They're always looking for an uprising to put down.' Mollie leaned down towards Ogden, spoke in a lower, ominous tone. 'And the only reason I'm riding back to town's because it's where I left my gun.'

Ogden shook his head as though he'd misheard. Then he reached for his horse, started to haul himself up into the saddle.

Impulsively, and because it was what he was being paid for, Copper John stepped up to Mollie. 'Get yourself mounted up, like you been told.'

Mollie took a quick breath, reached for the plaited quirt that was looped around the pommel of her saddle. Quickly, and in one movement, she turned and lashed Copper John across his face. 'Don't you *dare* tell me what to do on my own range . . . *ever*!'

'Leave her be. Saddle up and get the hell out of here, now,' Ogden's voice brought the gunman around, eyes narrowing as he stared into the muzzle of the man's carbine.

'I ain't paid to care for you, Ogden, an' I don't really understand what all this is about,' Copper John started, the blood streaming brightly from the wound on his face. 'But you tell this girl she's that close to losin' her hide.'

'Reckon she knows that.' Ogden waved his rifle, then

looked at the others. 'All of you, ride to Bluestem and wait for me.'

Mollie knew then that conflict was inevitable. For a distracting moment she was glad that Ben Shoeville was in jail . . . out of harm's way.

'I think you ought to be gone, lady,' Ogden walked his horse up close to Mollie's.

Mollie shuddered with misery and futility. The Bolas boss's words had somehow expressed the fear that nagged her, that Hog Flats was against her, conspiring to keep her from warning Will Chalk. She was tired now, but she cantered along, not sparing a glance for anything or anyone.

After five minutes, she turned to Ogden who was still riding beside her. 'If I give you my word that I just want to see Henri . . . take him into town to the doc's, will you let me through?' she asked.

Ogden cleared his throat. 'No. You wouldn't mean it. You're too desperate.'

'How many men have you got working on Bolas for no pay?' Mollie continued.

'How'd you mean?' Ogden reined in. They were only a few miles from town now, and he felt it safe to let her continue alone.

'You know I have no money to pay riders. And you know I have four men working at the ranch . . . two of them crawling through Condor Pass. Ask yourself this. How would it be if *you* couldn't pay for *your* gunmen.' Mollie smiled bitterly. 'You think they'd stay for water and biscuits . . . for loyalty? No, you might be a winner in the here and now, Ogden, but sure as hell you're a loser at most else. Think on it.'

Ogden blustered for a moment. 'It's different. Have you considered how your saddle tramps got so eager for combat?'

'By encountering men like you, maybe,' Mollie replied dryly. 'You're tossing a rotten apple into the barrel.' She watched thoughts spinning uncontrollably in his mind. When he wheeled away and rode off, she sat there silently until he disappeared in the vaporous heat.

Without pausing to look at the town, Mollie rode on past the rough-hewn bridge. She turned right a few hundred yards beyond, struck out for the open range land where Will should be waiting at the line cabin. Knowing that time was running out, Mollie accepted she had to ride the tough way there.

15

Bruno Ogden's search was beginning. Will Chalk knew it as soon as he saw the Bolas riders gathering in the home yard of Bluestem. From the doorway of the line shack, he lowered his spyglass, turned to face the prospect of the land above and beyond. The foothills were a bleak territory strewn with tanzanite, stunt pine and shifting scree. The ice was thinly sheeted on pools of standing water, the snow-line no more than an hour's ride.

'Latch. We're moving out,' he said.

Henri woke up, raised himself on an elbow. With his other hand he fingered the crust of bandaging around his lower neck, forced his eyes to the gloom of the cabin. 'There was a time when this kind o' life went with the job,' he said with a grim smile. 'But nowadays I'm really too long in the peg. Do I thank *you* for all this?'

'You can if you want,' Latch answered. 'You only lost a pinch o' flesh. How you feelin'?' Latch crouched down beside the metis. Then he turned to look at Will, confusion in his voice. 'Move? We've only just got here.'

'Come see this.' Will beckoned Latch to the door, handed him the spyglass. 'You don't want to be hanging around when they get here,' he said. The Bolas riders were strung out now, a dozen men riding in single file, urging

111

their horses up from the flats. The sun glinted on the rifle barrels and saddle conchas, and it was quite obvious that Bruno Ogden knew where he was going.

'Does look like they know somethin',' Latch said.

'Yeah, sure does.' Will went back into the windowless shack and stared pensively at Henri.

'I'll saddle us up then.' As Latch spoke, he drew in his belt another notch, as if in readiness. 'An' always when I'm hungry.'

'Do you reckon you can hold out?' Will asked of Henri. 'We didn't have much choice getting you here. Now I'm obliged to ask.'

The Bluestem metis saw the openness in Will's face. 'From here on, you'll play hell gettin' anywhere without me. I know these hills better'n my own pillow.'

'Can you track into Bolas?'

'Like I said, there ain't a dead trail to someone with Indian blood.'

'Bolas?' Latch blasted. 'What the hell you thinkin' of now, Will?'

'Ogden's down *there* . . . or soon will be. Him and practically every one of his paid followers, by the looks of it.'

'Yeah, gotcha.' Latch went back to the door and stared out across the valley.

Will looked down at Henri. 'Of course there is a place he won't come looking. The man-made barrier.'

Henri's eyes brightened as he staggered to his feet. 'The headwaters o' the Cholla? That's where they shot Lew Redbone. I'll take you.'

In the following few moments of silence they heard the distinctive ring of a horse's hoof, the anxious whinnying of their own nearby mounts.

'Now *you* come see,' Latch said, pressing his back against the open door.

112

The approaching horse slowed down. Then it stopped and pawed the ground in uncertainty. Mollie Broad looked enquiringly at the three part-saddled horses.

Will cursed quietly. 'She'll make someone a good scout. Either that or a goddamn bell mule,' he said, removing his hand from the butt of his Colt.

Mollie was about to ask what was going on when her glance fell away to follow Will's outstretched, pointing finger. She saw the line of horsemen working their way up the slopes, quickly realized the appearance of a mistake she could have made.

'I didn't bring them,' she said as a response to her own thoughts. 'I waited until Ogden and the other two had rode on. For the best part, I used the old Indian trail.'

'Hmm, why not. I guess it's her neck o' the woods too,' Latch replied as they stepped into the sunshine.

'Well, we were just leaving,' Will murmured. 'I hope you can make it back the way you came.'

'I came to tell you that Mower's going to put Ben on the Whiterod stage, three days from now.'

'Three days?' There was no more annoyance in Will's voice. 'That gives us time.'

Latch grinned at Mollie. 'How do, ma'am. You can take a look at your Henri, as you're here. The fever's up an' gone.'

'Yes, of course.' Mollie spoke softly, averting her face from Will. At the door she looked back, saw the Bolas riders were lost from sight, then hurried inside. Ten minutes later she came out with Henri behind her. Will's attention was instantly drawn to the clean, fresh dressing, and he smiled. A fragment of lace nestled in the nape of the man's neck, showed up bright against the relative darkness of his skin.

'Thank you. Now we can all get going,' Will said.

'Yes, don't worry about me.' Mollie climbed into the saddle, adjusted her skirt and glanced from one face to the other. 'What shall I tell Ben?'

Will returned a poker face. 'Tell him Whiterod's not all it's cracked up to be. That he's not to worry if he doesn't get there.'

Mollie nodded once. She turned her horse and rode away, dejected at not being more involved.

A cloud rolled up over the mountains and blotted the sun. Dark shadows and meagre rays of sunlight scarred the ground, the valley faded into a setting of indefinite shapes and sizes.

Latch grinned. 'Well, if you ain't the darndest, Henri. You really ain't lookin' your best.' He held the horse until Henri was in the saddle, then he swung up on to his own mount. 'An' I'm gettin' too old for this,' he added.

'You wouldn't be if I suggested we ride to the Bello Hotel,' Will said. 'It's time we moved out.' Will heeled his horse and motioned to Henri. 'Break us a trail.'

Henri kept away from any sign of a trail. He rode miles to avoid crossing a cattle track, slowly leading the way across the mountain borders of Far Creek. It was first dark when the juniper stands appeared. The three men ducked into the welcoming gloom, the tang of resin, working their way towards the roar of water up ahead.

'The Cholla.' Henri slid wearily from the saddle, looked up at his companions. 'So what do we do now?'

'What we came here for.' Will kept his voice down, led the way silently through the thick duff, with nothing but the sound of water to act as guide. 'Ogden used dynamite to collapse the bank in over the logs. I'm hoping there's a stick or two left over,' he said.

'We go to Bolas?' Latch asked.

114

'No. He won't keep explosives anywhere near there for an enquiring lawman to find,' Will replied. 'There'll be a cabin, a tool store.'

'An' how'd you figure on gettin' across that stream?' Latch asked. 'The rain's been here ... water's up an' runnin'.'

Will turned his face to the sky, felt the flecks of rain in the air. 'It's still here,' he replied. 'And a sierra storm would do the job for us,' he added thoughtfully. 'But we can't wait. I'll use the dam ... go across the top of it.'

'I can crawl pretty good right now,' Henri said. 'If there are any guards they won't see me. If they do, I'll be lookin' like a fat ol' log.'

'What's our chance of gettin' away with this, Will?' Latch asked. 'The truth.'

Will crooked a smile. 'At best, not good. At worst, zilch. But then I'm always hoping to get lucky.'

Henri checked his big Army Colt, pushed it securely back into his holster. He took off his hat, and re-tied his bandana loosely around his neck to cover his dressings. 'There. You ever work with dynamite before?' he asked.

Will shook his head. 'How about you?'

'Powder man with the Great Northern. Came to Bluestem from the Yellowstone. I'd say I just got elected for the job.'

Henri started to move off, held up his hand as Will attempted to dissuade him. 'I'm a Broad rider with a Bolas hole in him, so I won't be talked out o' this. You understand?'

'Yeah,' Will conceded. 'I was going to suggest we do it together,' he said, just as resolute.

With Latch using the spyglass to keep an eye on the landscape below them, the three men worked their way to the crown of the Cholla. The creek was wider with higher banks. Less than a mile upstream, the fluffy spume heads of water boiled into the excavations. They could see where the rock slide had stripped the mountain to bare bedrock, formed the main holding for the log jam.

The Cholla was choked with tons of rock and scree, below it the dam had backed up the waters to form a small lake, which raced out of sight around a bend in the hills.

If there were guards, a skeleton crew, they were nowhere to be seen. But wagon tracks plainly led down into the far reaches of the canyon. Will sized up the rocky terrain between him and the dam. To be seen on that slippery, mossy slope would be dangerous, but time was running out and they had to take a chance.

'We'll cross one at a time,' Will said, and checked his carbine and the cylinder of his Colt. He skittered downhill towards the dam, for a time belly down, sometimes crawling. He went on cautiously until he was at the brim, above the dropping wall of the Cholla. He looked down on the upper side of the dam, and in the clear, still water saw the logs and branches, rock and rubble which created the outer bulwarks.

Will pointed down, turned and motioned Latch and Henri to get closer.

Moving up, Latch turned his weathered face towards Henri. 'This ain't much more'n a wily ol' beaver's den.'

'Yeah. Knock out its legs, an' *pouf!*' Henri described with a short waving lift of his arm.

Will pondered his next move. An attempt to rush in could mean taking a bullet from any guard that Ogden kept posted. Then there was the canyon guard. An exchange of gunfire would bring the man out, or, worse still, send him straight after Ogden to bring back the Bolas gunmen.

'Can't be any shooting,' he whispered, his voice nearly

drowned out by the growling water, the increasing hiss and patter of rain through the trees. 'We'll split up . . . get them before they know we're here or how many of us there are.'

'I hope they're not sayin' the same thing about us,' Latch muttered back. 'If they're not stickin' to drive times, maybe there's somethin' hot on a plate. Let's go find out.'

Will grinned. 'That's your mission in life, Latch. Food an' drink. Bean master in a joint of the finest fixings.'

But Latch didn't hear. He was crawling across the dam, towards the high bank on the other side, moving snake-like towards the food and coffee smells he imagined drifting through the trees.

16

A blanket of mist spread down from the peaks of Condor Pass, and Bruno Ogden shifted uneasily in his saddle. He'd placed a ring of men around the shack, and Deavis and Copper John were inside.

'Deavis,' he called out.

'No sign of 'em,' Deavis replied from the open doorway. He held up a dirty, discarded handful of bandage. 'Looks like someone got their damage taken care of.'

'Goddamnit,' Ogden climbed from the saddle, his slicker gleaming, hugging his legs. He looked hard at the surrounding land, back to Deavis who was indicating back into the cabin.

'There was four of 'em . . . can't be certain,' he said.

'Three. Three men and a woman.' Ogden corrected impatiently. He walked into the shack and flared a vesta. He knew that Mollie Broad had been there, could almost discern the imprint of her boots. 'She was waiting, or more probably came in later,' he added. 'Timely enough to carry a warning . . . help her trusty retainer.'

'What do you want to do?' Deavis asked.

'Not waste any more time.' Ogden's voice was edgy again. 'They're up here, all right. I can almost smell 'em.'

He walked outside, peered into the damp cling of mist. 'But where?'

Two riders approached, their horses steaming and breathing heavily. 'There's sign, boss. One horse headin' towards White Mesa,' the first man said.

'That'll be Mollie Broad,' Ogden replied with little satisfaction.

'Remove her,' Deavis drawled. Then he caught the expression across Ogden's face. 'You may be sorry for runnin' up against this Will Chalk hombre,' he added less ominously.

'Why'd you say that?'

'It's goin' to be a nightmare findin' him in this, an' he knows it. Like a dust devil.' Deavis jerked his head towards a long, dark cloud nudging the peaks. 'Right now, we don't know where he is, but he sure as hell knows where we are.'

'Your point? You've obviously got one,' Ogden pressed.

'Bring the girl in, an' they'll come to you,' Deavis continued. 'Why put up with this when we can all get hunkered at Bluestem?'

'Not Bluestem. At Bolas.' Ogden pulled the neck of his slicker tight, then the front brim of his sodden hat down over his eyes. 'Take someone and bring her in,' he said, turning to look at Copper John. 'We'll ride back across Far Creek.'

An hour's ride away from the line shack, the chill rain seeped into Ogden's bones. The tang of wet horse beset his senses, his jaw was aching, his teeth starting to chatter. And it was galling to stare through a break in the mist, see the flats bright with sunshine. When they came to the timber, every low-lying branch flicked its water across his hands and face.

'If we stop at the dam, we can at least get a warm-up.' Deavis lifted his hat, slapped the rain from it.

'OK. Tomorrow, take the men you need and gather that Bluestem herd.' Ogden's tone had dulled a bit. He looked at Deavis, snorted at the inquiring look. 'Get the girl to Bolas and the beef to Mower's pens. We'll get it moved on before anything else.'

Deavis was about to interrupt, changed his mind.

'Yeah, near a thousand head of scrawny stock, and I want them off my hands.' Ogden said, as a rumbling noise echoed through the trees. Fine showers of water showered from the branches, and he dragged on the reins as his horse crow-hopped at the thunder.

'That's all we need,' Deavis remarked. 'Reckon it's the end o' the goddamn drought.'

Ogden ducked his head, cursed and rode moodily on.

Latch tied the catch ropes together, jerked the knots and grinned at the two Bolas guards. 'Huh, don't know about servin' up biscuits an' gravy,' he muttered. 'Seems I've got me a gift for parcellin'.'

Not understanding, the restrained men looked at each other and shook their heads.

'Those ropes could hold a half ton o' beef. Should be enough to stop you turkeys from goin' anywhere,' Latch added.

Henri walked from the guards' Sibley tent, his face serious. 'I think you're wrong about this, Will. Why don't you let me do it?' he asked.

'You'd be a sitting target if your neck or your back suddenly snagged.'

'Who from?'

'The canyon guard, if he came along. We can't take the risk.' Will ducked into the old army tent, and dragged a box outside. 'Everything here ready?'

'Sure,' the man confirmed, lifting the lid on sticks of

dynamite nestling in a bed of sawdust. 'I've set a three-minute burnin' time.'

'That's enough is it . . . three minutes?' Will picked up the box, looped its rope handles through the end of Latch's line.

'If it isn't, you'll be back up here a lot quicker'n you went down.'

'Now, tell me again. We all know this ain't a goddamn rehearsal.' Will stood at the rim of the dam, staring down into the canyon beyond. He was attentive to its depth, being lowered down on the end of a line with a case of explosives.

'Scrape a hole big enough to take most o' the box,' Henri repeated. 'Mix up enough mud to cover the lot. There'll be plenty of it down there. An' give us time to haul you up before you light it.'

'Water won't put it out?'

'No. Chinese use it on the railroad to blow up lakes an' redirect rivers. It'll burn OK.'

They waited until Latch had returned from along the opposite bank to fetch the horses. Wrapping the pommel end of the line securely around the saddle horn of his own mount, Latch nodded. Will handed over his hat and started his descent. Minutes later he reached the canyon floor, the line slackened and Latch eased off paying out the rope.

Will's hands were raw by the time he'd made a hole for the dynamite box. He knelt in the muddy soil, feeling the cold eat into him. The canyon was dark and gloomy, and looking up he could almost feel the press of low, heavy rainclouds. Grabbing handfuls of the mud, he pounded out an adobe mix, plastered it around the box and drew out the fuse. After what seemed like a full day, he laboured back to the high wall of the creek, stood breathing heavy and thoughtful with a vesta in his hand.

If Henri had miscalculated, there'd be no easy escape from the Cholla. Lighting the fuse could be Will's last hurrah, depending on how fast Latch could pull him up. If the rope remained intact, Will knew he'd be well battered and brusied long before being hauled over the rim of the dam.

He cast a quick look around, look upwards as he jerked twice on the rope. He struck the vesta and held it down to the fuse. For a second nothing happened, then the glow of the wick brightened, fizzed as the black powder caught, starting its relentless journey towards the mudbank at the foot of the dam.

There was still slackness in the rope and Will tugged impatiently, at the same time wondering if he could stamp out the fuse. He cursed, took two paces towards the fizzing light, then the rope tightened and jerked him off his feet.

Within moments the world was spinning, his mouth filled with thick, salty blood. He was bouncing against the logged wall, going skyward. He was still dangling in mid-air when he heard the roar of the explosion, felt the dam tremble and burst against his body. Clumps of earth, shards of rock and timber sprayed him, and then the water struck.

It seemed like he went under all at once, swallowed whole in the thunderous, roiling mass of water. *Can't see, can't feel,* he thought, *tossed around like a dead sprat.* He wanted to breathe, knowing the one thing to finish him would be a lungful of cold water. *Drag the goddamn rope in,* he was thinking when the uprooted bole of a tree struck his leg. Involuntarily, he gasped at the pain, then he was half out of the water, cursing, his eyes, nose and mouth full of the onrushing current.

On the bank, the rope turned into the trees and Henri watched and waited, tracing Will's movements with his skinner. 'I've got you feller,' he rasped, the long blade of his knife slashing down through the rope.

Will reached out, with both hands, pulled himself on to the soggy mire of the bank. He rolled on to his side, breathed deep, bringing control back, easing the shivers.

The two men sat side by side, nursing their own immediate thoughts. Both Will's hands were clawed with tension, his face was bruised, one eye was half closed, fluttering with a taut nerve. Henri's neck and shoulders were fiery with pain, but he was also feeling guilt.

'I guess three minutes weren't long enough,' he offered uncertainly.

'No,' Will agreed. 'Not by half a goddamn lifetime.'

Will didn't move until Latch came stumbling through the timber. He clambered to his knees, coughed and shoved himself upright, stood shakily staring at the Cholla. Now it was in seething, white-capped flood, rushing down the fissure towards the flats and Bluestem rangeland.

Different movements and noises made them take a step back from bankside. They looked up in time to see the two Bolas guards pushing their horses away through the trees.

Will cursed and smiled wearily. 'You made a good job of tying their hands, Latch. Shame you forgot their feet,' he said. 'But it don't matter,' he added with a shake of his head. 'They won't be giving us any more trouble. A couple of hours from now they'll be swimming the Rio Grande. Hell, with you and Henri's skills we've got nothing more to fear.'

'Yeah, sorry Will,' Latch replied. 'Somehow we've got out of our usual territory,' he added with a touch of irony. 'So where are we headed next?'

'Well, the line shack's off limits, and Ogden's certain to have sent someone to Bluestem to wait for us. And Ben Shoeville's on his way to a hanging.'

'Looks like there's options, then.' Latch picked up a pair of burlap sacks and swung them over his saddle. 'While you were down there playin' mud pies, I got us a grub pile,' he said and swung into his saddle.

'We're goin' for Ben?' Henri asked.

'Yeah. We stay away from Ogden and his men for a couple of days, then we rob the Whiterod stage.'

17

Ogden's voice was sour as he surveyed the wreck of the dam. 'That'll be the end of the drought for Bluestem. Those new men she hired have fooled us real good.' He turned on Mal Deavis, face darkening with anger. 'You should have got them. You had the chances.'

'Everythin's easier lookin' back, boss. You know that.' Deavis nodded across the river. 'An' what were the guards over there doin'?'

'I'll goddamn find out.' Ogden turned upstream until he could make a crossing. The creek was running out of its collected mass, and long sandbars were getting exposed. He held a tight rein, encouraging his sorrel across the sand and gravel. The other riders rode behind, horses' hoofs noisy as they slurped from the grasp of the water.

They came to the camp, sat in thoughtful silence looking at the trampled mess of the old Sibley tent. The fire and Dutch oven had been kicked over, good-riddance style, and the horses' picket pins were gone. All plenty evidence of the guards' hurried departure.

Ogden sat unmoving. His angry eyes stared into the middle distance as Deavis and his men searched around the camp. When they didn't find anything, Ogden rode to the edge of the dam, looked at the mass of foaming water as it raced towards its irrigating of Hog Flats.

Deavis rode back to the camp site, pointed up into the hills. 'That's the way they're headed,' he said.

'Do you know who they were?'

'I think so, yeah.' Deavis consulted with the others for a moment. 'Koons an' Lippet . . . your latest hirelings.'

Ogden lifted his chin and stared at Deavis. 'If you were aiming to get out of the territory, disappear by using some lonesome trail, where'd you go?' he asked.

'If I was desperate enough, I'd ride to Smokin' Snow,' Deavis answered. 'No reason to go there by choice. It ain't nothin' but coons an' wildcats. One saloon, one store an' no law.'

Ogden grunted. 'Good. But I'd like to know what's going on here. First, Sheriff Foote, then Mower starts throwing his weight around, now this.'

'Don't ask me, boss. Could be it's somethin' personal. But why don't we just get goin'? Them boys'll probably run till they drop, whichever direction.'

'Yeah, and do their goddamn blabber when they get there.' Ogden jiggled his reins. 'OK, the rest of you head back to Bolas. Deavis, you come with me.' He heeled the sorrel towards the trail of the fleeing guards. 'I want those two silenced. Let's go visit the wolves.'

An hour later, Ogden reined in. He turned in the saddle, with a hand on the sorrel's rump, looked back towards the Bolas ranch below him. Most of Hog Flats reached out in unbroken, ochre-coloured reaches as far as the horizon. He had a moment of anger because the Cholla was now in flood, adding salt to the wounding of his pride.

They rode in silence, cutting across stony basins, climbing to the rising foothills of the San Andreas mountains. It was where the snow lay deep in winter, pine-oak grew thickly, its needles soft and mushy underfoot. It seemed every branch flicked and trembled, alive with small, disturbed critters.

At first dark, with the horses stale and tiring, they picked out the blink of a few yellow lights ahead.

'Smokin' Snow,' Deavis said.

It seemed a long time before they actually approached the small, plain township, and when they did, Ogden remained in the lee of the trees, studied the collection of ramshackle buildings. He fleetingly pondered on how the place got its name, noticed a handful of trails branching from a single through street.

'One of each, you said.' Ogden laughed harshly. 'Well, it's a town that ain't prospered.'

Deavis was watching the Bolas boss peer through the branches of a pine. They were both mindful, melding with the darkness of the hills, estimating, listening.

Halfway along what passed for the town's street, someone walked from the shadows of one of the buildings, led two horses to a crude water trough. At the same time, a man appeared on the raised deck of the saloon. He took a long, sweeping look around then stepped back through the swing doors.

'That was one of 'em, an' that's their horses,' Deavis said quietly.

Ogden considered for a moment. 'You come into town from the far side,' he said. 'Give me time to get into that saloon – dog hole, whatever they call it.'

'Sure.' Deavis pulled his mount's head around. 'Then what?'

'You know what. I'll be inside. And bring your carbine.'

Ogden watched Deavis ride from sight before he walked his sorrel into the town. He looped the reins to the wheel of a broken-down cart, checked his shoulder rig and ambled to the deck of the saloon. He paused, checked on Deavis's position, took a deep breath and went inside.

The two men saw Ogden's reflection in the hanging mirror and for the shortest moment their world stopped. Koons attempted to suggest an indifference that didn't escape Lippet. Both men turned slowly, a calculated move away from each other, towards either end of the short bartop.

Ogden's glance flickered down to their empty holsters, and he had the confidence to smile. It was an acceptance of the sarcasm in Deavis's remark regarding his employment of them.

'I've seen the Cholla dam . . . had to guess at what happened,' he said with restrained challenge.

'An' that's what brought you up *here?*' Lippet asked defiantly.

'Not exactly, no. I came to ask why you didn't report back to me. I *am* the person who's paying you.'

'We didn't have time, an' we ain't takin' what we ain't owed. We're leavin',' Koons said.

Ogden shook his head long-sufferingly. 'You might have to rethink that.'

In the immediate silence, Ogden remained standing in the doorway. There was the faintest of draughts, the pungent smell of horses and sweat emanating in waves from Koons and Lippet. Their clothes were stained dark, scrubs of beard covered their faces. But Ogden knew they were as cunning as coyotes and their pups.

'A bottle and cigaritos, over here.' Ogden watched the barkeep push his order across the counter. 'Now we can talk,' he said nodding to the two men. He led the way to a table, pulled out a chair and sat with his back to the door. He coolly watched them pour their own drinks and light up the smokes. 'So where were you heading?' he asked.

'West, presumably.'

'Yeah. A long way west o' the big river, anyways.' Koons spoke for both of them. 'It's got to be one hell of a lot safer than workin' in this neck o' the woods.'

Ogden stretched his legs and listened. Lippet leaned back, relaxed his shoulders at the more comfortable manner of his erstwhile boss. He was thinking that, played carefully, there was still the chance of a getaway. Koons apparently was of the same mind. He stood up, but was too anxious and kicked over his chair. 'Reckon we'll just continue on our way,' he said tentatively. 'Arizona's a long ways off.'

'Like I just suggested, feller. You ain't going anywhere yet.' Ogden held the man with a chilling glare. 'Finish drinking.'

'What *did* you come here for?' Lippet asked, a hint of worry just beginning to show.

Only Ogden's distrustful eyes moved. 'Those two Johnny Newcomers you ran into, and the metis 'breed? Well, they're big trouble, and I still need good men.'

Lippet moved the bottle in circles on the table top, watching the shapes it made in the dried grime. 'I accepted fightin' wages Mr Ogden, but not for goin' up against any kind o' dynamite.'

Cutting through the weighty, explicable silence in the saloon, a booted footfall sounded out on the front deck outside. The barkeep looked up, dropped his wiping towel, his face taut as he backed off along the bar. Koons looked briefly at Ogden, then reached for the whiskey bottle. Lippet drew in his legs, more defensive than readiness for attack.

Ogden moved for his gun at the same time Koons reacted. Koons held the bottle, waved it in a short, sharp arc to spew the whiskey into Ogden's face. The Bolas boss

129

gasped, and Lippet shoved the table hard, sending Ogden crashing over backwards in his chair.

Koons saw the chance and leapt. He jabbed his knee into Ogden's throat and reached for the Colt, clawed it from Ogden's grasp as it left its shoulder holster. Koons used it to shoot out the big oil lamp, then he emptied the cylinder into the doorway as the doors swung open.

Lippet made his move towards the bar. He held out his hand. 'Get me your shotgun,' he shouted at the barkeep, holding out his arm, stretching his fingers. 'Now, for Chris'sake. Give it to me.'

But Mal Deavis was in the room and he fired his carbine. The first bullet hit Lippet between the shoulders, the second lower, shattering his spinal cord. The stricken man collapsed, face down in the dirt that had already accumulated in tiny drifts across the saloon floor.

Koons saw the shape of Deavis framed against the front window. He stepped up against the side wall, peering into the gloom near to where Ogden had fallen. He sensed rather than saw the man come to his feet, heard the whoosh of the chair as it was hurled from the floor to smash into the big hanging mirror. Ogden's shadow crossed the doorway, then suddenly stopped, still and resolute.

'I don't have a gun.' Ogden's voice broke across the claustrophobic room. Koons made a run for bar cover, the shotgun he knew must be still there, somewhere.

'Take this.' Deavis lobbed his Colt through the hang of burnt cordite towards Ogden. Before it fell to the floor, Ogden caught it, and using both hands, levelled up and fired.

Koons took the bullet high in his chest. He spun around, slowly sank to the ground, his fingers releasing their life's grip on the apron of the terrified barkeep.

'You still alive, son-of-a-bitch?' Ogden spoke sharply from near the door.

'He's here . . . dead.'

At the sound of the barkeep's troubled voice, Ogden shot a warning bullet into the low ceiling. 'Stay where you are. Don't move a muscle,' he ordered.

Deavis struck a vesta, lit a pair of happy jack lamps on a side wall. Ogden turned to the barkeep, waved him away from near Koons's body. 'Take a look,' he said to Deavis.

Ogden heard the sound of broken glass, and when Deavis nodded he looked back to the barkeep. 'From now on, choose your customers more carefully,' he advised. 'If you don't like their look, shoot 'em . . . feed 'em to the pigs. It could save you a lot of time. Worse still, having me return to burn you all down.'

Without another word, and Deavis close behind, Ogden picked up his Colt and hurried out to his horse.

18

It was full dark when the two men reached Bolas. Ogden heaved himself into his den, sullen faced and tetchy. He stood for a moment in the dark, head lowered, watching rainwater trickle down his slicker. Then he sensed the strange vulnerability of his back, became aware that he wasn't alone.

He let his hat fall from his left hand, slid his right into his Colt. He drew back the hammer, was drawing the gun from its holster when Preston's Mower's voice cut the gloom.

'Did you find them? Did they find you?' There was clear anxiety in the trader's tone, a catch of fear.

'No. We didn't find one another.' Ogden was brusque, ignoring Mower as he laid his nickel-plated Colt on his desk, peeled off his slicker. He sat down heavily, pulling irritably at one of his boots.

Mower lit the wick of a decoratively glassed oil lamp, flicked the vesta into the fire duff.

'Make yourself at home, why don't you?' Ogden muttered, unlocking the drawer of his desk. He pulled out a bottle of bonded whiskey and a glass, poured a big measure and downed it in a single swallow.

'You want to lay off drinkin' it like that,' Mower nagged.

'Wouldn't be so bad if it was donkey piss.'

Ogden fought back the gnawing retch of an empty stomach. 'It's more profit for you, goddamnit.' He slammed the glass on to the table, stared at Mower with tired but hostile eyes.

'It's only 'cause I care for the liquor,' Mower twisted a smile.

'Wit don't suit you, Mower.' Ogden stood up and walked around the room. 'So get serious and figure out how the hell you're going to water the beef next year.' He waited a moment. 'Our log jam's been blown to Texas,' he said, when no response came.

'We can build another one.'

'*You* can build another one,' Ogden rasped. He slammed a bunched fist down on the table, grasping the whiskey bottle as it toppled. 'Far Creek and Bluestem won't need it. But *you* will . . . Bolas will.'

'You sayin' they're dead?' Expectation suddenly flared in Mower's eyes, died again when Ogden shook his head negatively.

'Hell. You're movin' out. Is *that* what you're sayin'?'

'Not entirely. I'll move off Bolas, and on to Bluestem.' Ogden gave a humourless grin. 'And that reminds me. Get your stock pens ready. I'm sending you a tally of beef that needs getting rid of.'

'No,' Mower stated bluntly.

'You can sell it on the reservations. You've done it before.'

'That's as maybe. But no more,' Mower repeated, sweat glistening across his forehead. He grabbed his hat and took a step towards the door. 'I've got enough to handle with Ben Shoeville.'

'Shoeville?' Ogden repeated and picked up the bottle. He tipped it towards his glass, stopped short when he heard an angry murmur of voices rising from the yard. 'Wait up,' he said.

The two men stood facing each other, listening to the force of Copper John's voice, the sound of boots scudding on the veranda. There was a sharp battering against the door and the Bolas gunman entered. He didn't see Mower as he pushed Mollie Broad into the room ahead of him, to Ogden's chair.

'There you go boss. Quicker'n ol' John Butterfield,' he said, grinning wickedly. Without waiting for a response, and with his back still to Mower, the man turned on his heel, closing the door firmly behind him.

'Mower! Why didn't I think. . . .'

Ogden saw the incredulity in Mollie's eyes as she looked around her. He watched the sudden uneasiness twist Mower's features, the sag of the jowls.

'Remember,' he said. 'We're starting the gather in the morning.'

Mower's face darkened as he stared back at Ogden. 'I've said all I'm goin' to on that score,' he ground out. He levelled a finger at Mollie, his other hand stretching for the door behind him. 'Now you'll have to get rid of her.'

'Hah. I'll let you do that.' Ogden's voice was spiky. 'A task maybe easier than the others. I'm thinking of her father, and Turner Foote, and Ben Shoeville, even. Hell Mower, you're a real paladin. But I wonder if any of those unfortunate folk were facing you.'

Before anyone could stop her, Mollie shoved herself up from the chair. She reached for the desk in one swift movement, grabbed at Ogden's Colt.

Mower wrenched the door open. He took the veranda steps in a stride, fled into the darkness pursued by Ogden's jeers. Out on the trail, trying to make sense of his predicament, working on his next action, he didn't know that

Bruno Ogden was standing with his foot placed firmly between Mollie's shoulder blades. She was being held down, her face lying sideways in the rain-wet slicker she had tripped over.

Mower kept up a hectic pace back to White Mesa. He'd sensed the fear that drove Turner Foote to call time, was now gripped with real worry. And Ogden was in a mood to spill the story to Marge Highgate. Mower cursed long and hard when he considered the consequences of her learning the truth of Elmer Broad's death. He understood her antipathy for Mollie and everything Bluestem, and that she wouldn't hesitate in seeking an appropriate end for the murderer of Mollie's father.

Mower left his tired horse ground-hitched outside the mercantile and rushed inside. The accumulated dust of varied dry goods lifted from the puncheons as he stomped huffily across the floor.

'First thing in the mornin' hitch up the springboard,' he told the sleep-in sales help. He headed for his office, stopped in his tracks as the door opened before him.

In the wedge of yellow lamplight, stood Marge Highgate. 'Where've you been at *this* hour,' she demanded roughly.

Mower coughed, braced his legs and straightened his back, carried on through into his living quarters. 'Bolas, to see Ogden . . . thought night-time was best. There's a lot of stuff to get cleared before I take Shoeville on that Whiterod stage.'

Marge Highgate glanced quickly around the room before settling on Mower. Her instinct suggested immediately that he was still in the throes of a big scare. 'Tell me, Preston,' she said less harshly, 'How'd you know who it was killed our sheriff?'

The three men had made camp in the concealment of a scrub thicket a half mile above the White Mesa-Whiterod stage road. A steep-sided hogback lifted to where timber provided cover for a man to covertly watch a long stretch of road. Beyond that, a slope ran down steeply to the Cholla, now moving fast and muddy.

By inclination, Latch was up early. He brewed a pot of coffee and put together a spare breakfast, stamped out the last spark of fire.

Lying in his saddle blanket, Will peered up at the fading glimmer of stars, the appearance of a false dawn across the San Andreas Mountains. He propped himself on an elbow to take the steaming can of coffee.

'You reckon Henri'll make it?' he asked.

'Yeah, I'm damn sure he will,' Latch replied. 'All them Red River bloods are made o' jerked meat.'

'We can't afford to get trailed,' Will said after a mouthful of warm biscuit. 'We'll lose ourselves in the big timber . . . surprise 'em. That's our edge.'

Latch was thoughtful. He hunkered down, half watching the trail. 'For a one-time lawman, you're mighty relaxed at carryin' out an armed hold-up,' he said.

'Justifying the means, Latch. On the other hand, some say the difference between banditry and the law's only paper thin.' Despite his sharp reckoning, Will *was* troubled, but it was more about Mollie Broad and Bolas. He rolled from his blanket, stood up and smiled reassuringly as Henri came through the trees.

'My worry about the hold-up is that Mower's filled the coach with deputies . . . a passenger posse,' he said.

'If he has, they ain't goin' to be much more'n saloon swills,' Latch replied. 'No. No honest citizen's doin' squat for Preston Mower. Let's go rob a stage.'

Full daylight broke through Condor Pass. Will was on a track he had worked out with the others after smashing up the dam. He had estimated they would get the first glimpse of the stage when it splashed from the creek, headed towards the hills.

They pressed on through the trees until they came to a high point directly over a turn in the mountain road. In front of them, a big overhang of rock with a petrified juniper attached, perched on the edge of the barranca.

Henri impatiently kicked away loose stones and clumps of weathered twig. Latch picked up a sturdy branch, jammed it into a wide split and started to lever upwards. A wedge section of the boulder shifted a little, teetered forward then levelled itself back again. 'Should've kept one o' those thunder tubes,' he said.

'It's not the rock. It's the roots of the old tree,' Will replied. 'Been dead fifty years and still won't let go. Be careful. We don't want to be going down with it,' he grinned earnestly, helped twist the branch further into the crevice.

The slab of boulder didn't move until sweat streamed down the faces of Will and Latch. Then, and still in the clutch of the tree's carcass, it shed grit and stones, angled over the rim of the barranca to the road below.

Latch gulped. 'Jeez, if that big passel o' dirt actually hits the coach there'll be nothing left for us,' he rasped.

'That won't happen,' Will said. 'Just get yourselves down there and see the coach doesn't drive around it. I'll take care of what happens next.'

Will waited until Latch and Henri were in position either side of the wagon road, then he, too, backed off to watch from cover. Minutes later he heard the crack of the driver's whip, the urgent shout as he drove the horses up the gradient.

When the Concord coach appeared around the bend in the road, Will heard the screech of its brake blocks. Immediately, he walked to the nearside rear wheel and stepped up on to the hub.

The driver grunted displeasure, leaned over and called to his passengers. 'We've got trouble. I'll need a hand out here.'

Latch walked into the road, his rifle aimed up at the driver. 'I come with the landslide,' he said clear and loud. 'Climb down nice an' easy.'

Inside the coach, Mower eased back the roller blind, fumbled at his belt and drew his Colt. 'You stay put,' he told Shoeville. 'It makes no difference to me how you get delivered . . . alive or dead.'

'It matters one hell of a lot to us.' Henri was standing on the off-side step. He smiled tightly at Shoeville, saw the handcuffs and pushed the barrel of his big Army Colt hard into Mower's back. 'Just drop the gun, monger man,' he commanded. 'Or I shoot out your spine . . . supposin' you got one.'

Mower opened his hand, let the gun drop. He was looking out the door of the coach, more or less facing the gun of Will Chalk.

'You,' he ground out, his eyes ablaze with threat. 'Hell, do I rue the day you walked into my store, Chalk. But now I'm puttin' a price on your head. I'll deputize every man in White Mesa . . . Bolas if I need to.'

'Oh, you'll have to, Mower,' Will replied. 'I've heard about the quality of your proposed deputies.'

'You best scuttle home,' Ben Shoeville spoke up. 'An' stay behind the counter. I'm goin' to look into Sheriff Foote's death, an' when I find out who did pull the trigger, you'll be first to know . . . I promise.' He held out his hands, shook the handcuffs. 'Now unlock these, you son-of-a-bitch.'

The mercantile owner-town sheriff, smiled coldly. 'You're clear out o' luck there, mister. I ain't carryin' the key. Since leavin' White Mesa, it's only the marshal in Whiterod can take 'em off. Reckon you can see why.'

Will reached out. He bunched the front of Mower's shirt in his hand, twisted and dragged the man from the coach, down to the roadside. 'Empty your pockets and take off your boots,' he rasped.

Mower got to his feet, pointed a thick finger at the driver. 'You knew this was goin' to happen,' he accused throatily. 'You'll pay dear.'

The driver climbed down from the box, stepped straight up to Mower. 'Payin' dear's sure somethin' you'd know about,' he said thoughtfully before smacking him hard across the mouth. 'An' *that's* on behalf o' the townsfolk who have.'

Will held back an approving smirk and held out his hand. 'The key, or I'll be having *my* say,' he threatened.

Mower drew the handcuffs' key from his trousers ticket pocket, handed it to Will, who handed it to Henri.

Shoeville stepped down to the roadway. He massaged his wrists, backed off as Will pushed Mower back up into the coach. Henri nodded, held out the cuffs and clamped them on Mower. He grinned, and threw the key out into the roadside manzanita.

'Not to worry . . . we know where there's another,' he said quietly. 'Look forward to seein' you in court.'

'Take him back to White Mesa. And don't stop,' Will told the driver. Then he helped uncouple the horses to turn the coach.

Will, Latch and Henri waited until the coach was on its way back, out of sight around the bend, then they re-tracked the barranca, gathered their horses and rode towards Bolas.

20

They rode through the heat of the day. Henri's neck and back were stiff but there wasn't much pain. His eyes were keen and he continually quartered the hills for some sign of Bolas guards. Will and Shoeville rode together, Latch zigzagged the backtrail. To the east and west of Condor Pass, the country lay flat and shimmering in the bright sunlight, mesquite thickets stretched away in every direction.

Shoeville rode easily, but occasionally turned back, offering Latch a curious, uncomfortable stare. Tired lines etched his face, his eyes were restless.

'I know it's uneasy me watchin' out for you, Ben,' Latch eventually called out. 'But when a man's distracted, he'll maybe miss somethin'.'

'I'm not goin' to miss anythin' . . . like Ogden's gunmen, if that's what you're worried about,' Shoeville returned quickly. 'I didn't think I'd have to tell you that.'

'You didn't. *I* was just tellin' *you.*'

They all rode a while in brooding silence, then Will spoke up. 'So, who does what then?' he asked.

Shoeville stared ahead to the rising trail. 'If anythin's to be done, it's more my place to do it. Perhaps that's what I was thinkin' about,' he replied. 'But I can't bring myself to kill if it's the wrong man.'

'I'd like to think that of us all,' Will said. 'As sheriff, Mower can arrest Ogden, but he won't. He's already

140

warned us he'll pin badges on all the Bolas riders.'

For a few minutes there was more quiet time, disturbed only by the dull clip of hoofs, the jingle of bridles, creaking leather.

'Right now, I'm as close to bein' an old man as I'm ever likely to get,' Latch said. 'With less at the end than anyone else, why not leave it to me? Hell, after all this, I'm near one o' the Bluestem family.'

'An' have the folks in Hog Flats think the ramrod's gutless?' Ben Shoeville's eyes narrowed, the muscles along his jaw line twitched. 'If Ogden does manage to stay alive, we might as well find another state to live in.'

Will flashed a meaningful look at Latch. 'Looks like judgment time,' he said. 'Bluestem or Bolas. There's no room for both.'

Ogden's valley headquarters was the low-lying ranch house, surrounded by buffalo berry fencing and arching willows. Corrals, barns and outbuildings rambled across the broad slope behind the house. The Condor Peaks rose majestically from a rangeland mix of snake bunny, daisy and lush grass.

The Bluestem riders dismounted in the trees. It was where the canyon plunged, almost a sheer drop to the floor of the valley. They tied in their horses, approaching on foot until they got within rifle range of the ranch house. The windows and doors of the house were already open, wood smoke curled lazily skywards. Nearby, a juniper railed corral contained the restless movement of seven saddle horses.

Will pulled his rifle from its scabbard, walked slowly towards the lip of the canyon. He sat cross-legged, pulled the brim of his hat down, rested the rifle across his hips.

A man appeared on the surrounding gallery of the house, picked up a bucket and walked to the near empty creek. Behind him, the early sun lifted like a flame from the hills, pierced the trees and heated Will's shoulders. His mouth was dry from tension, and gently and quietly he levered a cartridge into the chamber.

Bruno Ogden came out. He stopped on the porch and raised his head, observant for danger, a difference. As he scanned the surrounding hills, he looked directly to where Latch and Henri were hunkered, then he turned away.

While Ogden quartered the land, Shoeville lifted his rifle and took slow, careful aim. With the butt squeezed hard against his shoulder, he nuzzled his cheek to the stock. The rifle felt cold and hard in spite of the rising warmth of the day, and he took a breath. He squeezed the trigger back, taking up the slack, lined up the front and rear sights.

Sweat now leaked from every pore, his eyes smarting in the brightness of the light. His hands started to tremble and it spread to the rifle and then back to his whole body. He knew he could still fire and hit Ogden high in his chest . . . couldn't miss. But he held the final pressure on the trigger. 'You'll never know it, Ogden,' he whispered. 'Whatever time you've got left's down to me.' Slowly he lowered the carbine, felt Will's eyes on him.

'I can't kill him like this. That's for others,' he murmured. 'I want him to know it's me.'

'Sometimes it matters,' Will agreed. 'Later. We'll wait till he's in the open.'

Ogden walked into one of his clinkered barns, reappeared a couple of minutes later leading a chestnut mare out towards the trough.

'Christ, that's Mollie's horse!' Shoeville got to his feet as he spoke, but Latch made a grab for him, pulled him back down to the ground.

'Keep down, else none of us'll see the day out,' he rasped.

'There'll be bad killin' here if they've harmed a single

hair of her head,' Shoeville warned with palpable emotion, and Latch shared a discerning look with Will.

Mollie Broad sat silently watching Ogden, who in turn was indifferently listening to the sound of voices from the corral. She had been like this for a long time, refusing to acknowledge the man being there or to answer his questions. Occasionally, Ogden stared back, the shadows dark across his troubled face.

Sometime between first and full dark, a man entered the room from the kitchen. He walked with the uneven gait of a horse breaker, ignored Mollie, spoke straight to Ogden.

'Help's in from Bluestem. Thought you'd want to know,' he said.

Ogden turned his head, stared absent-mindedly. 'Right,' he replied with delayed comprehension.

The stove-up wrangler's glance passed over Mollie, then he turned away, left the room the way he'd entered.

Still preoccupied, Ogden paced the room until he heard Mal Deavis calling for him.

'Beef's gathered,' his man said, as he stepped down from the saddle. He looked at the open window, indicated that Ogden move away, and lowered his voice. 'The stage never made it to Whiterod. It came back . . . empty 'cept for Mower.'

Ogden cursed, thinking that Mower was selling him out. He calculated that while the Bolas crew were waiting for Bluestem to come and get Mollie, Mower had gone to Marge Highgate. 'Lickpenny trader,' he muttered. 'OK, I want that beef in the pens by daylight. Give the son-of-a-bitch a herd of blotted brands to explain away.'

'An' what about the girl?'

'What about her?'

143

Back in the house, Ogden unlocked his gun rack. He selected a Colt revolving shotgun, loaded it and put four extra cartridges into his pocket. Feeling the burn of Mollie's scorn, he turned to face her.

'Leave Mower. He's for me to deal with,' she seethed. Mollie's attitude was unexpected, but Ogden didn't listen. He went to the front door and shouted.

'Deavis. Find some help and get in here.'

Minutes later, Ogden spoke to Deavis and his crippled hostler. 'Secure her and keep her quiet,' he instructed. 'I'll be back soon as I can.'

He led his sorrel from the corral and saddled it, slid the shotgun into the scabbard and mounted. He rode north, splashing through water that was coursing in from Cholla Creek.

Darkness came and still Will had no plan. He saw Mal Deavis leave the house several times for a walk around the yard, but all he and his partners could do was lie unmoving in the brush, watching the house like opportune foxes. Oil lamps were lit and weak shadows fell across the home yard. Will knew that if they waited much longer, the initiative, their surprise, would be lost.

'Bring in the horses, Latch,' he said. 'We'll walk them down, off the rim.'

From the deep, shadowy gloom of the trees, Shoeville took the reins from Latch. He flinched when a night owl decided to screech its alarm, cursed as a distant coyote started its moonlight howl. 'Goddamn critters know there's somethin' up,' he muttered.

'Yeah. Gives me the jitters. I always think it's personal,' Henri said uneasily as the porch lamps at the ranch house went out and silence smothered the brush.

Shoeville and Will stood close in the darkness.

144

'You and Henri stay with the horses. Me and Latch will go on in,' Will said quietly.

Shoeville shook his head stubbornly. 'I'm goin' with you. Don't try an' keep me out o' this, Will. We'll have our own fight if you do . . . seriously.'

'You're in no shape,' Will whispered. 'You nor Henri. For Chris'sake, you'd both be a liability. No disrespect.'

'The hell with that.' Shoeville pushed Will away. 'Me an' Henri have been sharin' mescal buttons in case you hadn't noticed. We won't be feelin' much of anythin' till Mollie's safe.'

'Ah, stop your gabbin',' Latch said sharply. He pointed towards the Bolas ranch house where the silhouette of a man showed clear against a window blind, as a lamp was lit.

'They know we're here . . . must've heard somethin',' Henri whispered. 'I'll calm their horses while you go on in.' He shook his head at Shoeville. 'Not yet. Let 'em go. It's best.'

Most parts of Will's body stung as the brush scoured him in his dash to the rear of the house. He saw the back wall, a door, windows either side. He glanced around, saw Henri and Shoeville emerge from the bunkhouse, wave their hands for them to go ahead. Then Latch was beside him and they stepped into the enveloping atmosphere of a ranch-house kitchen.

The darkness was intense until their eyes adjusted and objects took on shape and form. They stood very still, taking in the cling of old woodsmoke and grease. They had no way of knowing when Ogden might return, and before they could make a move, a rifle shot cracked out, then another, and glass smashed.

'They're comin' through,' Deavis shouted. 'Watch the back door.'

Will took a few steps forward, kicked open the door that

led to Ogden's office. He saw the shadow of a man coming fast towards him, the gleam of a firearm. But Latch pushed him aside as more gunfire flashed in the gloom. He heard Latch gasp as he was hit, saw the running man lower his shoulder in a charge, and bring Latch down.

The gun hands of Deavis and Will moved together and the house rocked with more gunfire. Mollie's voice shrieked above the noise, the sound of her fists beating wildly against another door.

Will steadied his Colt in a two-handed grip, aimed decisively and pulled the trigger.

Deavis took the bullet in his chest, stumbled as the dark stain spread across the front of his shirt. He half turned, fell against the end of the big desk, gasped and raised his head. His features were warped with pain, sweat gleamed across his forehead. He muttered an oath at Will, moved his gun defiantly and drew back the hammer.

Will fired again and the gunman grunted, buckled into a heap on the floor. He tried to get to his knees, was staring down at his hands as his arms gave way. 'What's it to you?' he mouthed into a fold of the big Navaho rug, then died.

Latch stood up slowly, looked down at the body of the Bolas gunman. 'Should've dealt with beef,' he grated. 'Hell, Will. I think I heard some angels sing just then.'

Shoeville came into the room, held up his hand as Latch struck a vesta to light the lamp. 'Where is she?' he asked anxiously.

Will turned the latch-lock of the small store room, and opened the door. Mollie almost fell through, almost into the arms of Shoeville. Her hair was loose and tousled, her face drawn with all sorts of alarm.

'Did they hurt you?'

'Not hurt, no,' she replied. 'I'm all right. But Preston Mower was here. Ogden said he murdered my pa. He shot

146

Turner Foote, too.'

Will saw the dismay in Mollie's eyes. 'Where did Ogden go?' he asked.

'They're driving my beef into Mower's pens. Him and his crew.'

'Mower, Ogden and Foote,' Shoeville's voice rasped with understanding and anger. 'That's them ... the Bruno Ogden Land and Stock Company.'

'Maybe. But we've to prove it,' Will murmured.

'We will,' Shoeville said. He looked at the desk, pulled out the drawers. 'It'll be here somewhere. There's got to be papers an' documents.' He tried the drawer above the knee-hole but it was locked. He cursed, stood back, raised his foot and kicked at the handle. The drawer sat firm and he cursed again before shooting the lock.

Sitting in Ogden's chair he pulled the lamp towards him and leafed through packets and papers. The air was heavy and hot, pungent with low, curling smoke. He took off his hat and flung it down, pulled the crook of his arm across his face. He glanced at the tally sheets, his frustration and anger rising.

Minutes passed before he found the legal document neatly folded inside a Bolas accounts transaction book. He read slowly, looked up at Mollie, his eyes expressing incredulity.

'Do you know Marge Highgate's writing?' he asked.

'Yes. I think so. What's that to do with anything ... all this?' Immediately, Mollie wanted to yell. An explosion of feeling, like a statement of the obvious. 'Why do you ask, Ben?' She repeated.

'Because, according to what's here, she owns a quarter share of the Bolas company. She squares the circle.'

21

Marge Highgate pushed open the gate in the low picket fence and walked to her porch. She stood a moment, half turned and looked thoughtfully towards the Todo Mercantile. There was something going on with Preston Mower that she couldn't put a finger on, and it worried her some. Half concealed by the rambling honeysuckle, she sat in the rocker and watched the street. Presaging the downpour, a few drops of rain fell, ruffled the dust in tiny craters.

Minutes later, she stared at the rain-driven night. The rocking got slower, stopping altogether as her rambling thoughts became unexpectedly fearful. There was something that passed between Mower and Ogden she didn't understand . . . something Mower refused to talk about. And she wondered if it was happenstance that the trader was at once so panicky.

Ben Shoeville's out there, she thought. *Him and three others. But it's not that . . . not Bluestem he's scared of.*

She manoeuvred her chair back out of the wet, her mind still on Mower. Then it came to her. Slow at first, just an undertone. Then it held, and started to build. *Turner Foote's no longer with us. And soon the Bruno Ogden Land and Stock Company will be in the hands of one man . . . will have grown into its name.*

Marge cursed at the thought and stood up. A real gully washer was now sweeping the town. Big teardrops of rain splattered the growing channels and pools of mud. A flash fork of lightning was closely followed by a crash of thunder that shook the house. It pressed and rattled the windows, and Marge cursed again.

Then there was another kind of trembling in the ground. Something was approaching across the range, and Marge recognized the sound of a running cattle herd. Animals frightened by nature's elements sounded like they were headed straight for White Mesa.

Now Marge shaped oaths that were more explicable, more fulsome. She heard crazy barking of the town's pariah dogs, assessed the fearful beeves to have already reached the ox-wagon camp on the outskirts of town.

She went into the house and found her slicker. In the parlour, she opened a cabinet, took out a derringer pistol. The weapon was blunt-nosed, carried a single .38 bullet and was effective for up close and personal work. She hurried back out into the night, extinguished the porch lamp and bowed her head against the slanting rain.

Approaching Todo Mercantile, Marge saw a horse she recognized, watched for a moment before stepping behind the cornerpost of the store's freighter landing. When the sorrel came closer she saw the rider was Bruno Ogden, and had to hold back from reacting. Then there were sounds from inside the mercantile and Mower pushed open the big screen door.

'Are they here?' Ogden called out.

'Who?' Mower answered, pushing the door shut.

'Will Chalk . . . Shoeville . . . any of them. Who do you think?' Ogden reined in beside the raised boardwalk, the water dripping and sliding from his hat and slicker.

Mower stared at him speechless. The rumbling thunder crashed around the town, near drowning the gunfire of the Bolas riders as they contained the running herd.

Ogden stepped down into the mud and hitched his sorrel, oblivious to the storm and Mower's nervousness. He ducked under the rail and stepped up to the trader. 'You must've heard,' he said.

Mower stood with his back to his store, gun hanging limply from his weak fingers.

'You're like one of them three goddamn monkeys, Mower,' Ogden rasped. 'You've got a gun in your hand, for Chris'sake. You must be expecting something to happen. Chalk and Shoeville took Mollie Broad. They busted my spread, then rode on to the drive, and set it to flight. The storm did the rest.'

'I told you not to bring the herd to my pens.' Mower's voice was bitter and rash. For a moment he forgot Ogden, was concerned solely for his own immediate wellbeing.

'Well, it's happened,' Ogden stated. 'It would take more'n any General Jackson to stop them now. Look there.'

Pouring from the creek hollow, near to a thousand steers were on a lumbering run. The herd wasn't yet stampeding, but it filled the breadth of the street, bringing down hitch-rails, veranda uprights and overhangs, veering left and right into every path and alleyway.

'Keep away from here.' Mower raised his gun, aimed it at what appeared to be the leading beeves. But Ogden struck his arm away, shoved the trader back to the wall.

'Save it. You're going to need all the ammo you've got when Chalk and Shoeville get here,' he rasped. 'After you've tried to talk yourself out of your past doings.'

Squeezed in between a side wall and two big flour barrels, Marge tried to hear what Mower and Ogden were saying to each other. The first bunch of beeves had lumbered past and the shortest lull followed.

'You're a damn fool to come lookin' for trouble if the Broad girl's free of Bolas,' Mower said.

'Yeah? She was a lot goddamn safer with me than her father was with you,' Ogden retorted sharply. 'He was found face down with a bullet in his back. Your bullet, Mower.'

Marge heard the door open, had a look to see the two men walking into the store. She came out of hiding as the main body of cattle, with their wet, shaggy heads lowered, were milling into a tighter circle. Using a clap of thunder for cover she hurried inside the store, silently kneeled behind the counter. With Turner Foote dead, together with his valuable cover of the law, a feeling of uncertainty welled up in her. Now, she thought she had somehow been outsmarted.

It became obvious as she watched the slant of persistent rain through the window, that she was through in White Mesa. She had been for many years, arguably since Elmer Broad's death, with a chunk of hatred and self-pity to feed off. She had yearned for close, personal company, but the door to that had long been banged shut. Banged shut, and bolted by Preston Mower and his rifle.

From underneath her slicker, Marge eased back the hammer of the pocket pistol and reached for the mercantile office's door knob. Mower was sitting at his desk and Ogden was standing by the window. Curiously enough, Marge felt nothing but a stony emptiness at the sight of them.

Ogden considered Marge with guarded curiosity as he stepped back into the room. He glanced at Mower, who tensed like a coiled rattler. 'Hah, the men need a gather, almost as much as those goddamn beeves. I'll go see to it,' he said. He moved towards the door, halted when Marge held up her hand.

'No, you won't.' With a faint smile of contempt across her mouth, Marge pushed back the hood of her slicker, revealed pale, drawn features. 'You stay right here. Bolas is having its last board meeting.'

In the small office, the tension was stretched tight. Mower inched back in his chair, sized Marge as someone about to need a coffin. But her look slashed him like a whip. He looked to Ogden for help, saw there was none coming.

'You're a greenhorn in this neck of the woods, Mower,' Marge continued. 'The Highgates and the Broads fought just about anything that could move for this land. That was in the days when your store would've been Davy Crockett's privy.'

Mower peered at Marge across the light of the lamp. His right hand moved to rest beside the gun belt on the desk. 'Spare us the history, sister,' he returned. 'What are we goin' to do?'

'Do? We?' There was open scorn in her voice now. 'If you're still breathing at first light, you'd best be doing it from the other side of the Llano.'

A dark, angry flush crept across the trader's face. Marge's forewarning had cut deep. He knew he was holding the weakest hand, albeit the one he had dealt himself. 'Bluestem's got a lynchin' planned. Tonight,' he offered.

'Well, they can go right ahead. They can hang the man who back-shot Sheriff Foote. If that satisfies them,' Marge said flatly.

'An' what would satisfy you?' Mower asked. But his eyes flicked to Ogden.

'Seeing *you* on the end of the rope.'

Mower didn't move, but his hand was close to the holstered Colt and his fingers flinched. 'Take it easy, Marge. We're *all* in trouble here,' he said. 'Something's gone wrong, an' if we don't stick together, we could *all* hang.'

'Like hell we could,' Marge snapped. 'The best they can prove against me is a part share in Bolas. I'm no murderer. Not yet.'

The two men then saw Marge had a gun in her hand, that it was pointed directly at Mower's face.

'But by all that's legal, I'm soon going to be,' she continued, her voice calmer, cooler. She leaned across the desk top, water dripping from her glistening chin, tendrils of hair against the sides of her face. 'You shot dead Elmer Broad. It's for *that* I'm going to kill you, nothing else,' she said. 'I'd like to have done it a long time ago . . . but I never knew until now. Not really.'

Mower twisted awkwardly, pushing himself away from the desk. In a kill-or-be-killed moment he grasped his Colt, hooked back the hammer.

Marge Highgate's gun exploded. The bullet struck Mower between the eyes, tearing a neat hole before taking out a lot more at the back.

Mower pulled the trigger as his head was hammered backwards. But he was dead long before he hit the ground, his body half trapped beneath his own big chair.

Marge stood poker-faced, her hand dropping to her side. 'When I told my ma I was headed out west, she told me I'd probably come to a bad end,' she said, her voice now thick with emotion. 'She was nearly right.'

Ogden was breathing deep, staring unfocused down at Mower. 'He was a murderous son-of-a-bitch, Marge. Good job you were facing him,' he said, as if justifying the action.

Marge walked slowly across the room, lowered herself into a chair. She blinked back reality, let her eyes close as she listened to the shooting and the cattle bawling, dogs barking in the street.

The outer door opened and slammed shut. Ogden drew his Colt, from his shoulder holster, levelled it across the office.

Copper John appeared in the doorway, his clothing caked with mud, watery blood streaming thinly across his face. He stared at the body of Mower, then at Marge, then at Ogden and the nickel-plated Colt.

'What the hell happened here?' he breathed.

22

The lamplight from the Bello Hotel floated and flickered across White Mesa. The rain-lashed main street was empty now, except for the debris left by the wild running herd.

The storm had transformed the nearby creek into a torrent of water that now washed across its bankside boulders. A few wagoners who had been sheltering beside the rough-hewn bridge drew aside, let the four horsemen advance unhindered on the town road.

'Might be difficult, but no shooting until we get real close,' Will said. 'And remember, they're hard men ... probably won't let us fire twice.' He looked at Mollie Broad and shook his head. 'You're staying here, boss lady ... ma'am.'

'What are you going to do?' Mollie asked, her concern mainly for her ramrod, Ben Shoeville.

'Look for Ogden and Mower. What else?' he said. With a wave of his hand he indicated that the other three cover any movement in the main street.

As they neared the mercantile, a flash of lightning lit the townscape, revealing three riders advancing towards them.

One of the Bolas men urged his mount ahead of the others. 'Where are you fellers goin'? An' who are you?' he called out.

'We're Bluestem,' Shoeville shouted back. 'As if you didn't know.'

'You're not wanted here. We've orders to shoot you,' the Bolas rider warned.

Shoeville gave a derisory snort and put his horse straight at the man. He drew his Colt, swung the long barrel at the first slickered rider.

Will and Latch sprang their horses to the left and right of the group and started shooting. It was an army cavalry tactic, calculated to demoralize and disorientate as much as kill. Horses squealed and quaked, reared in fear. A gleaming dark bay slipped in the mud, fell to its knees before rolling and disabling its rider.

Will saw Shoeville firing as he knee'd his horse in a tight circle. A Bolas gunman was returning intense fire, but he was the one who fell. He crumpled forwards, then toppled sideways down to the ooze of mud. Shoeville lost control of his own horse, and they both pitched forwards threshing, gasping breath in the pelter of rain.

Henri rode in, shouted something to his horse, before swinging down from the saddle. He grabbed Shoeville's leg, dragging him free of the stirrups, and the dying animal. He crouched down close to his wounded partner, cursing. 'Come on, bring your Bolas guns,' he yelled. 'We're down here waitin' for you.'

Will looked back, saw the blurred shape of Mollie urging her mount up from the bridge. Ahead, at the Todo Mercantile, the two horses were stamping, nervously shoving each other against their hitches.

'Ogden's inside,' he warned as Latch rode up beside him. 'Reckon they'll know we're here.' He could see a side window, a weak rectangle of light. 'Like moths to a flame,' he added with a grim smile.

Will dismounted, eased his holstered Colt and started towards the store. Gaining shelter of the loading platform, he untied the two horses, sent them on an eager, veering run into the rainy darkness. He glanced at the irregular run of lighted windows along the street, wondered if the townsfolk would stay safe until the noise and general mêlée was over. He saw Henri walking towards them, his gait made more awkward by the suck of greasy mud around his boots.

'So let's go fight. You first,' Latch said and followed Will up on to the mercantile's covered landing.

Edging along the clapboarded walls, Will came to the front door, warily looked into the gloomy interior. He could see the long, stacked counter, the slice of light that showed under the door along the rear wall. He stepped into the store, wondered about the murmur of voices that held no hint of identity or purpose. The shortest moment later he cursed silently and crossed the floor.

In the office, Bruno Ogden was holding up a document in his left hand. His face was flushed, his lip almost curled with pleasure. 'I can only guess at what's going on out there,' he started. 'But for *this*, I'm obliged, Marge. In signing, you've granted me all four shares in Bolas. So whatever happens next. . . .'

Before Ogden could finish, the door crashed open. From the darkness of the store, Will caught the lamplight, sensed it almost blinding. Then he saw Marge Highgate turn her face towards him. In the same moment, from looking over Ogden's shoulder, Copper John let out a roar of anger and flung himself away from the pool of light, his hand reaching for his high-belted pistol.

Ogden let the papers fall. Without rising from the desk, he lifted his right hand and fired in one, fast movement.

But Will had the advantage of preparation and surprise.

His bullet hit Ogden in the middle of his chest, slamming him back into the chair, a surprised, futile look already etched into his face.

Will knew the gravely wounded man could still bring him down. He jerked to one side, almost tripped on Mower's body as Ogden's Colt fired. Then Latch and Copper John were firing at each other and Will cursed loud and wild, felt a sliver of dread as Latch stumbled to the floor across the doorway.

With his chin dropping, Ogden raised his Colt in both hands and fired again. Will felt the pulse of air as the bullet passed close to his neck. He turned sideways on, raised his right hand and shot calculatedly at Ogden's bloodied chest. The dying man jerked once and lapsed into total stillness.

Will shouted Copper John's name and swung his Colt into the low swirling haze of gunsmoke. But there was a noise like someone or something had blasted through a wall of the store. The shot wildly stirred the room and Copper John died trying to figure out what had happened.

Henri stood over Latch. He was grim and resolute, cradling his old Army Colt. 'Usually only needs the one shot,' he grated. The tall metis stepped forwards into the lamplight, looked contemptuously at the bodies of Copper John, Mower and Ogden. 'I guess Bluestem's done what it had to,' he said icily.

Marge Highgate remained slumped in the chair, too tired and depressed to do more. She stared dully, pulled long wisps of grey hair away from her usual tight bun. 'He killed Elmer Broad,' she said. 'It was him . . . Mower.'

Will heard her strained voice, saw the embittered shell of an old woman – the woman who'd loved Mollie's father for half her life.

'Trouble is, justice don't mean much when it's delayed

for so long. The son-of-a-bitch,' Marge continued, as much to herself as anyone else. She shuddered, raised her face to look at the bodies. 'What a price to pay.'

Will holstered his Colt, looked to see if Latch was OK.

'A lump on my head an' a cut on my leg. Hah, walkin' wounded, as usual. Nothin' that the Bello Hotel can't take care of,' Latch said.

'Well, there'll be no more fighting. Everyone's dead,' Will murmured. He looked again at Marge, wanted to say she wasn't included, but he didn't. 'Let's get away from here,' he offered instead.

Marge raised herself from the chair, stooped to pick up the paper that Ogden dropped. 'I'll take this with me,' she said. 'There's an erratum I need to take care of . . . some re-alignment. I'll get it to young Mollie when it's done.'

'Why? What is it?' Will asked.

'A deed. At the stroke of a pen, Mollie Broad's going to own Bolas. But she'll probably want to change that name.'

Henri and Latch followed Will down the street to where, oblivious to the rain and mud, Mollie was kneeling beside Ben Shoeville.

Grimacing at body pains, Shoeville raised himself as the three men approached. 'Henri, you ol' goat. You left me here to die, goddamnit,' he growled.

'I didn't mean to,' the metis replied. 'I thought you were dead already.'

Mollie shook her head, smiled at Shoeville. 'You once told me you wouldn't rest until I was safe with Bluestem. Well I am, so you can. God bless you, Ben.'

'An' there's one or two cows to round up an' take home,' Henri added.

A small crowd had gathered on the broad stoop of the Bello Hotel. They were restless, anxious, sharing thoughts on the night's events. Latch coughed, licked his lips,